INFERNOMEISTER

Duncan Cullman

authorHOUSE®

AuthorHouse™
1663 Liberty Drive
Bloomington, IN 47403
www.authorhouse.com
Phone: 1 (800) 839-8640

Published by AuthorHouse 11/27/2019

ISBN: 978-1-7283-3796-8 (sc)
ISBN: 978-1-7283-3794-4 (hc)
ISBN: 978-1-7283-3795-1 (e)

Library of Congress Control Number: 2019919360

Print information available on the last page.

This book is printed on acid-free paper.

RONALDHINO

10:34 AM

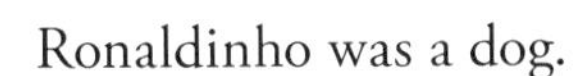

Ronaldinho was a dog.

His dog mother gave birth to him under a ski area cafeteria halfway up the ski slopes of Cerro Catedral, Alta Patagonia, Argentina.

When he was born he had no name at all other than puppy Cachetorrito. "Arf,arf, arf," his mother called him with some barks.

Though for the simplicity of this story we will call him Ronaldinho because that is the name he received later in his life.

His mother dog was so hungry from pregnancy she had eaten some discarded chocolate bars left in the snow by very rich spoiled children from the capitol, Buenos Aires.

Later while nursing her puppies she ate another chocolate bar, not good for dogs because of the caffeine, not good for the puppies drinking her fresh milk with caffeine. The poor little puppies all became hyperactive and nervous to the extent that when the cook owner came to collect them and sell them at the market for a few Argentine pesos, Ronaldinho ran away into the mysterious beech forest on the high mountainside, El Bosque.

His mother dog came to nurse him once and tried to carry him back down the mountainside but he was already too heavy so she left him some discarded bones to chew. The young puppy was destined to be a wild dog.

Meanwhile a wolf mother lost one of her pups possibly to a condor, she was searching all night and day for it frantically when she discovered Ronaldinho whom she mistook for her own thinking he might have rolled in Guanaco turds as he now smelled different than her own pups but not much different.

But being a good wolf mother she brought the straggler puppy home to her wolf den where another of her puppies was now missing. At least she had Ronaldinho to nurse and mother.

So the young dog was very fortunate to have a mother at all since his own had gone with the cook to market in San Carlos de Bariloche, the nearest city. The cook became drunk on Chi Cha and lost all his money in a card game that lasted past midnight when supper was served.

The wolf mother brought all her cubs to a higher wolf den on Cerro Pillin on the other side of the mountain Catedral which is Vuriloche. The young Ronaldinho now became a tactical hunter in the footsteps of his mother. They ate shrews, moles, mice, marmots and sometimes dead things frozen in the snows of Pillin.

Once they even ate a dead skier who had skied a closed backcountry trail in the fog and had fallen off the backside of the mountain Catedral into Vuriloche. He was a big fat Porteno with a spare tire of lomo meat around his gargantuan belly. His family didn't even report him missing as he had spanked his wife and children continually so they did not miss him one iota.

Naughty big and naughty. The wolves and Ronaldinho now a wolf thought the fat porteno to be very delicious. Munch, munch, munch!There were many animals in the forest and fish Truchas in the ponds, lakes and rivers plus pumas (cougars) and condors and sea birds from the Pacific Ocean not to far away in Chile.

"What big eyes you have," said Ronaldinho to his wolf mother.
"All the better to see you with!" replied his wolf mother.
"What a big nose you have!" said Ronaldinho to his wolf mother.
"All the better to smell you with," replied his wolf mother.

One time they all discovered a giant Puma (cougar) standing over a freshly killed deer. There was blood everywhere in the snow.

The wolf mother growled hungrily so all the now bigger wolf pups growled to be like her and they were just as hungry. After a few more bites the Puma decided to abandon her deer meat as there were just too many wolves to tangle with. So the wolves moved in to share what was left of the dead deer, letting Mother Wolf have the first bite of many. Even the bones were eaten. Much, munch, munch.

Sometimes the hungry wolves even ate insects by licking them up with their tongues. Slurp, slurp, slurp.

The very next winter a snowboarder fell out of the sky it seemed and landed eye to eye with Ronaldinho. Both were surprised! After exchanging glances the snowboarder whizzed off down the mountainside.

There was a moon which seemed to talk and make faces through the clouds so every wolf and dog as well howled at it for its reply. There were comets and countless stars in the cold and freezing coyote nights. Then one day Ronaldinho's wolf mother lay down and was motionless with her eyes still open and her tongue stuck way out of her mouth. She did no longer breathe and her eyes then glued shut and her body grew cold as the snow and rocks. She died.

All of her wolf children howled all night long to the angry moon which now shed some rainfall tears. One by one Ronaldinho's wolf brothers and sisters wandered off in different directions to different adventures hunting in Villa Angostura, El Bolson, Maiten and valley of the Black Glacier of Cerro Tronador.

So Ronaldinho was all alone now, he had never felt this lonely. So he began to search for a mate, a dog who might remind him of his mother Wolf or even his birth mother dog. There were some dogs at the base of Catedral Ski Mountain, even some Huskies with yellow and or blue eyes which are like wolf eyes. One of them had eyes like his wolf mother.

The two of them began to play at first in a game of I can catch you but can you catch me? This was very amusing to them and even spectators watching from a distance, very competitive also. Ronaldinho had to demonstrate that he was healthy and quick, fast and strong: that he would be a good father soon to her newborn puppies.

He was indeed. So they fell in love, Ronaldinho and the Husky sled dog and they ran away together up the slopes of Cerro Catedral into the snows of Pillin and Vuriloche. There she found a den for her puppies that were soon born and healthy.

But one day a Puma came and killed her and ate all the puppies while Ronaldinho was off hunting for Condor eggs, trout and deer carcasses.

Then he returned home to her den and there was blood everywhere and his beloved was dead just like his wolf mother.

So Ronaldinho went down to the base of Catedral because he was starving and heartbroken. He had lost his entire family. Then a lady named Lynn came out of the building Salon de Te and brought him some leftover pizza the rich Portenos had left on the table uneaten to show off their great wealth. Then Lynn's father Ramon saw Ronaldinho from inside the steamy warm windows and brought him some bones and leftover meat.

Now Ronaldinho had a new home and people to love him even though he barely knew what love was he sensed it was very good indeed not like Pumas. He slept peacefully by the door but inside while skiers came and went, some asking questions about the dog that acts more like a wolf in the doorway.

"We named him Ronaldinho!" proclaimed Lynne and Ramon when asked. Ronaldinho was very fortunate to have a home as there are so many homeless dogs everywhere in Latin America. They live near restaurants and near bus stations and in the streets near markets and trash thrown into the street usually in plastic bags which they rip apart with their teeth to find tasty morsels. Very sad this is indeed because all that plastic blows in the wind to rivers to the ocean which kills fish and seabirds.

Then one day a foreigner tourist came to Salon de Te and his name was Ronaldinho. He was very rich and famous from Brazil where he played soccer. in the World Cup. He signed many autographs and starred in a movie. He asked Lynn what is the name of the dog in the doorway that looks more like a wolf and ignores everyone.

"O that is Ronaldinho named after you!" replied Lynn with Ramon's approval," But he has had a very hard life in the mountains as he was mostly wild but now has chosen to come live with us!"

The movie star athlete wanted to pet the dog but Ronaldinho just growled at him. "He doesn't like strangers, "Ramon explained, "Some people wanted to buy him because he's part wolf and they wanted to pay thousands of pesos but he's not for sale as he belongs to himself. He's his own dog and doesn't need a master. He's an Alpha wolf dog!" Lynne explained

"Oh that figures," said a passerby snowboarder who owned a wolf in another village.

Then one day the snowboarder who had almost crashed into Ronaldinho in Vuriloche on the slopes of Pillin came by to visit Lynn and asked,

"Where is that dog by the doorway, the one you call Ronaldinho?"

"Oh I am most sorry," said Ramon adding, "He died last summer, a blue pickup truck ran him over on the road above here to the Tramway base. His face was smashed and he was just left to die there by that heartless drunk borracho. I found him and buried him by the big rock on a quiet path nearby I can show you"

"Oh how sad said the snowboarder. A year later the snowboarder married Lynn and Ramon retired from the restaurant to live on a meager pension and go fishing in a river of tears.

They didn't have any children right away, Lynn and her snowboarder. husband. Maybe they were always snowboarding and too tired to hold hands and or kiss. So they decided to go to the pet store and adopt a puppy which had very big ears like Ronaldinho.

"What will you name this lucky puppy?" asked the silly lady at the pet store as she was so excited it would have a home.

"Ronaldinho!" exclaimed Lynn.

"Ronaldinho!" said the snowboarder at the very same moment.

The moon shone through the very fast moving windswept clouds of Alta Patagonia and seemed to be whispering to the little dog whose eyes were wild with excitement and he began to bark at it as it rose above the gargantuan Andes Mountains. They all lived happily ever after.

Completed as the omnibus stopped in El Bolson by the writer and storyteller Duncan T Cullman copyright 2015

1965

Tuesday, Nov. 17, 2015, 5:32 PM

In 1965 I was in South Station almost every weekend from Christmas until March. The reason being I was recovery from trauma inflicted by those desperate agents of evil, the men in black. The one that jumped upon the stage in the café was none other than the Angel of Death himself, Josef Mengele. He had actually been with ski troops in support of a Panzer Division sent to break through with supplies for the German forces of Von Paulus surrounded by soviets in Stalingrad. When one of the tanks was hit Mengele jumped upon its turret and pulled two burning kameraden from it saving their lives for which he received medals of bravery and loyalty to the FuhrerAdolf Hitler und Hitler ist Deutschland und Deutschland ist Adolf Hitler etc.

So Mengele went to the hospital back in Germany with burns and a broken ankle from his adventure and his professor contacted him with utmost authority to ensure a promotion for him should he accept a command at Auschwitz, a prison of war camp and much worse as history would reveal

Mengele went there after his recovery and because he had authority to save so many people for experimentation he also saved a tall young white Russian woman whose real name I am unsure of but her Israeli passport later gave her the name Mona Nishkin or something similar. Because she was like a girlfriend to him he saved her then hid her and she survived the war to go to New York and South America where she claimed to me she had recently seen her captor "The Angel of Death" himself wandering around Oliva,a suburb of Buenos Aires. Of course she insisted that I could help those (Israelis?) track him down because he was wanted for war crimes. I felt somewhat willing as it seemed adventurous!

So she insisted that at the end of my every ski run I should slow down and wait for the man on one ski with one leg who was constantly trying to catch up with me as he would probably offer to take me over the border to ski in Argentina. I was gullible and naïve, my father later explained to me that because they offered me nothing in return for a great deal, I never should have listened to her or them.

Water under a bridge now because I went to Argentina where the pilot insisted I take a room with the Syrian refugees from the war. Of course I had been part of that great meeting in the back servants' quarters of Hotel Portillo where communists and subversives made plans for any left wing cause. But I was told to leave the meeting early because if I were captured it would be better the less I knew.

So there in the Syrian auchluss escape house for all refugees from the war(on the losing Nazi side)I unpacked my things as it down poured so heavily suddenly one of the Israelis who had been camping demanded space on my floor. He insisted pointing his Berretta in my face.

The Nazis had eyes and ears everywhere and knew I had been visited by a subversive. So already I was a marked man boy and it would just be a short time before Rudel escorted me in his silver stainless 1953 Porsche to Skorzeny for questioning Argentine style.

They ask you the question then before you can answer they just hit you anyway, blood splattering everywhere, no fun at all, not even for a teenager. My jaw was broken: I couldn't talk anyway and then they decided to dislocate my right hip just for fun so I couldn't walk. Thrown into a jail cell I presumed I was left there to die when suddenly they brought one of the Israeli campers whom they had caught dozing in the rain soaked puma pampa.

They came to take him to interrogation asking him just who he was and he replied to those men in black.

"I am Jesus Christ sent to redeem your lost souls, in fact to save you from death and grant you eternal life. He was so very funny I almost laughed but then they shot him in a place where the wound was indeed mortal and he slowly began to die in the jail cell with me but luckily just prior to this he had put my hip back in its socket so I was beginning to recover somewhat and that's when he picked the lock and we escaped in darkness down the beach near Llao-llao the giant summer gambling hotel there west of Bariloche nine miles.

I had to tell him about when I first arrived there in Rudel's Porsche he had brought me upstairs to the grand Ball where a man who looked like Hitler grabbed me by the ear and said to the others,

"See here this year is just a trifle smaller than the other and this is why we shouldn't trust him!"

The Israeli was dying I was sure and he knew the wound to be mortal and he was rambling on incoherently about his family who had all been killed in the Seven Day war in 1956.He had lost them all but could hear and see them all dancing on a distant beach somewhere where he was going, and then he went there as he died turned to a cold stone after pointing his gun at me and saying I was one of them so he should shoot me!

I had to leave him and walked through some woods where I found a road and then out of nowhere it came with its headlights glaring a silvery Porsche and the familiar voice said,

"Get in. I'll take you to your hotel." I now had to go back to somewhere but I passed out cold from exhaustion.

SHOE ON THE OTHER FOOT

The shoe was soon on my other foot when I traveled to ski race at Chapelco with Janko Greztec whose father stayed home as he was a busy older doctor from the Polish Resistance of the Warsaw Ghetto Uprising... (The surviving Poles had surrendered honorably to Hitler who gave them honorable German citizenship whereas Stalin had double-crossed them) So we traveled by bus from Bariloche with Ski Club Andino to the Chapelco parking lot where Janko told them that I had a Jewish father. All the young athletes unloaded except for me and off they went up the mountain on two chairlifts to the ski race championship, a gala affair with hundreds of curious spectators in spite of the falling snow.

I was told that because I was a Jew, I was not permitted in the town of San Martin which was protectionist of its exclusive Catholic culture. It was very cold on the bus and I shivered as I was perhaps underdressed expecting a normal sunny ski day in the Andes with bright sun warming me at the high altitude. Of course, I never completely forgot this treatment by the otherwise friendly Argentines.

In the finals of the Olympia Beer Cup in Washington State at Alpental I was afforded a similar experience by Bob Beattie.

After I won two runs on alternating courses of giant slalom against Spider Sabich, Beattie, my former ski coach but now Spider Sabich's sports agent as well as tournament director (conflict of interest?) informed me that it was now officially changed to a four run final not the normal two runs. I won the third run in a row and returned to the starting gate above the television cameras and over a thousand spectators mostly on skis.

"I don't care how many runs this takes," replied Bob Beattie, "Spider is going to win this pro race. The sports writers have already written their articles and they are not rewriting them for you!"

In the fourth run at the count of three Spider Sabich bounded out of the gate so I left at "One" and at the finish line he was still five inches ahead so he was declared the winner.

Connie, my former ski companion from five years before, knew I had been screwed over as well as all the other pro athletes, but what could they do against the all-powerful dictator of ski racing, Bob Beattie?

I was happy to be on television and win $1,200 which in 1971 was a lot of money

We all went out for Chinese dinner and celebrated, a dozen or more at one table. I never won a ski race on World Pro Ski Tour and everyone now knows why.

SECRET SERVICES

My father confided to me over a quiet breakfast.

"You haven't done well at all in school and apparently have little or no direction in your life as far as a professional career but there is something you can do if you would like to volunteer for it. I can arrange for you to meet a professor at Yale University who specializes in recruitment for special services?"

I listened attentively as always to my father who had adopted me. God only knows what I might have become without his help. I liked playing sports and long weekend trips to Vermont in winter when we skied though rarely together. I was still a young kid at fourteen and a nit immature.

"Okay I'll do it!" I agreed to volunteer.

I arrived by taxi to a special office at Yale University. A maze of mostly white colonial buildings. The kindly professor admitted me into his office and explained that I was volunteering for a kind of mind control. I was nervous at first but soon agreed to hypnosis. I don't recall much of anything except that I was instructed to forget my briefing. I was to be sent on a special mission for my country.

THE SECRET LIFE OF LOUIS COLEMAN

Growing up in greater New York City I learned that delivery men were Italians, bartenders and cooks were Irish, dishwashers and field hands were blacks. Of course there were people who had shiny new cars and wore suits and ties and those were the English. My father instructed me that the English now ruled the world.

There were the French from France and they had been collaborators with Hitler and so had been expelled from the New Postwar France of Charles De Gaulle whom everyone in America detested as he wanted to withdraw France from NATO. There were French in Canada but those were mostly Indians descended from trappers who took natives for wives as no Parisian beauties could be found to freeze their delicate French asses in North America.

We lived in Fairfield County in Connecticut, a New England State that had originally been settled by the Dutch so it really was more like New York than Massachusetts.

My mother Thais was originally from Boston where she rode horses as a young girl with her sister Jean and Brother Ned behind their house in Hingham in a large apple orchard. I was very fortunate to be adopted by rich people and live in the richest nation on Earth, the United States of America which had just won two World Wars: and dropped the Atomic Bomb on Japan, game over.

Now there was lasting world peace in the New Order with the American President telling everyone in the world by radio and television (a new invention) just what that would be.

My father was a little bit different as he was Jewish and Hitler had just killed six million of his kinds. Apparently nobody liked them as they had too much money. My mother didn't seem to mind as she went shopping for groceries and the latest gossip.

Albeit about my father being different, he was white like his older sister Nan whose real name was Francis. When he was born his mother, my granny Wolfe, told him,

"I didn't want you!" He was born last of five siblings and she had apparently already had it, meaning she was fed up with everything from breast feeding to babies crying in the middle of every night every year for twelve in a row.

My father's poor luck to be the very last and unwanted. Even his own brothers didn't want him. Somebody started a rumor that my granny Wolfe was having an extra marital affair with some German who probably raped her in a taxi cab or limousine off in some forest who knows where.

So my father attended Choate, Hotchkiss and Yale in that order, having been sent away to boarding school at age twelve because of my granny Wolfe's guilty conscience or just because she was a lazy bitch or that's what my grandfather Joseph called her.

Joseph Coleman III was the son of Joseph Coleman Jr who my father never spoke much about as probably nobody liked him. The Coleman men were very tough on their women and children, scolding them constantly like Londoners. They had come to Cologne, Germany via London where one had managed to marry the red haired granddaughter of the Bishop of Cambridge, John Hall.

Some Coleman's had arrived on Ellis Island, New York as immigrants in the late nineteenth century and soon found work delivering newspapers on bicycles. They worked their way up to eventually become Coleman Bros., a respectable New York Firm including Philip Morris Tobacco, Benson and Hedges Tobacco Company and Marlboro Cigarettes. Joseph Coleman III was much enhanced marrying Francis Wolfe whose Dutch Indies family had relocated in Dutch Guyiana and actually knew the tobacco industry inside out.

My father's two older brothers Joseph IV and Edgar planned on cutting him out of the family business from day one B.C. before time even was invented. His brother Arthur managed to escape the family with a teaching degree and became the Dean of Ohio University.

My father actually thought he might be German as opposed to a Jew whose ancestors lived in Germany. Charles Lindberg flew a plane across the Atlantic Ocean and he was a sympathizer with Hitler. Germany was on the move ideologically and in mass production. Furthermore, the German people were the Master Race. So was my father also from about six years old onward.

So at Yale he joined the Bundes League of German Brethren who all drank beer and went skiing and sang German songs, although my father rarely sang because his voice was nasty.

Possibly at Yale his infiltration of the Bundesliga made him an attractive candidate for the U.S. Government which wanted to know who the sympathizers with Adolf Hitler were.

I only know there was a Bundes Book and a Browning automatic in the little drawer in the bed stand. I never asked him about it after mentioning it once as he said to me,

"You didn't see it!"

There was one particular acquaintance of my father, a tall man mostly bald with a few locks of blond hair and very bad breath who. apparently had no name. I was told that I never had met him and not to mention him to anyone. He was at Yale Bowl in the restroom coming up behind my father at the urinal. He was a cruel man with a very mean and bitter attitude because Germany had lost the war. We met him at some other person's house where I was told to go play in the yard. We met him again at llaima Volcano in Chile where he and my father talked extensively. I met him without my father on the chairlift at Alpine Meadows during the Junior National Ski Competition. He coached me well that day in spite of his cynical bad attitude on life in general. He told me to just ski down the course and make it to the finish line as most of the young ski racers would not as it was a blizzard. I finished sixth but won the next year at Bend, Oregon. I had finally escaped both my father and that strange man.

LOUIS B COLEMAN

Louis My Father

At the tender age of five my parents Louis and Thais informed me that I had been adopted and that they weren't my original parents whereupon I began calling them by their first names.

For a woman my black haired Thais was a real monster. Luckily she had a sweet disposition half of the time but the other half of the time when I refused to eat my burnt overly cooked lamb chops, she spanked me and tossed me back into my crib. So I too was a little monster in her image.

My father came home every evening from New York on the train (which I had yet to discover) and appeared at the back door which she sometimes locked as her lesbian friends were retreating out of the living room by way of the front door.

Then one day an ambulance came and they carried my mother out the front door screaming. She didn't want to go to that Sanatorium in Stockbridge, Massachusetts.

My father looked at me with terror in his eyes and proclaimed, "Now you'll do what I tell you to do!" Hardly.

So he took me with him to Washington D.C. where he applied for some government job in a very big building. I had to wait in a room somewhere until he returned Child abuse: they didn't have a name for it back then. You did what you were told or got beat up. In Sweden they were trying something new and experimental called child psychology but in America well here we did everything with B-52s dropped bombs on them all if they don't agree with us. Yes and if they might persist there was the Atomic Bomb. BANG!

On a casual drive through Jefferson, New Hampshire en route to see my grandmother Darthea in Mooselookmeguntic, Maine my father had to inspect a hotel that had been burned down by Sugar Hill resident Joseph Kiernan of the Boston Common Garage embezzlement scandal for the insurance money. My father wasn't very thorough because he explained to me that he didn't want that job with the FBI they wanted to transfer him to. He had a job with some other Department of government. I was very little still and didn't quite understand. We would go to Lexington, Kentucky to meet his boss and then to Germany France Switzerland Italy Spain: all part of his job. I never saw him work although he attended meetings. He had been a second Lieutenant in World War Two which he had fought in Algeria in a Weather Station making forecasts for the Invasion of Sicily etc and I was later to understand from my history books that that was a very big World War which we had won so I should be very proud of my father.

But deep down inside I was already a communist although not a registered communist. My father keep talking to our ski instructor Miki Hutter from Austria about Skorzeny's military exploits rescuing Mussolini etc but on television I saw Germans in uniforms and they were all the bad guys I thought, especially the Japanese. We were taught racism in school-to hate our enemies.

But in church we were taught to love our enemies. I had gone to a Danny Kaye movie with my mother before they carted, Frank was an avid her off. Wonderful, wonderful Copenhagen the movie showed how wonderful the Danish children were: I wanted to go there. My mother said they wouldn't like me there because my father was Jewish. It was a truly confusing world, especially for a little monster in the making.

But now my mother was gone and in her place there was a whole family of house servants, the Groves from London. Evidently my father sensing that since I was of English mostly extraction this stable family would be a good influence on me and he was right because Mr. Groves was an avid athlete gardner roofer soccer player and he soon coached the Masonic little league team starring his son Graham and me, while Mrs. Groves, Caroline baked chocolate cakes and cleaned our house.

I took Graham on a ski adventure when it snowed we went to the Country Club Golf course hill where he skied over a sand trap unable to turn and crashed head first yes blood and his mother wasn't too impressed grounding him.

I was eventually shipped off to a prep school in New Hampshire at age thirteen because I was continually fighting at school. That's when my father met a divorcee named Dorothy the Witch I thought. She was after his money but of course he didn't ever have any until his father's will was settled and then every bitch in hell. was turned loose and they all had a lot of makeup and ruby red lips and a lot of hair like my mother but they shaved it and wore excessive perfume. Disgusting to a thirteen year old.

Then I turned fourteen and it somehow all made sense. The Groves all became history for me as they moved to Narragansett, Rhode Island near the beach somewhere.

I went to Chile with my father where he met some tall bald man with a German accent near Llaima Volcano we all skied but the lodge was very Smokey and I got the flu while the adults climbed the volcano. The tall German looked a lot like our distant neighbor from Pound Ridge,New York who had beautiful blond daughters and golden retrievers. His wife,bald man invited me to come ski race in Argentina which was very orderly and so against my father's wishes I had boarded a train for southern Chile to join up with the Chilean ski team all young boys and girls with their chaperone Mrs. Leatherby, the wife of the owner of farellones Ski Area, Chile's very first. She had been a ladies golf champion of Chile under her maiden name Gazitua.

Over in Argentina I was to stay at the very friendly but not really very friendly at all Syrian Auchless or something Refugio for Refugees of the War (they lost) and an Israeli showed up with a gun. I had met him evidently in Portillo, Chile. Now I wanted to forget him: but the gun was loaded and cocked.

"Okay you can spend the night" I agreed.

My father's friend Doctor Little in Bozeman, Montana sent a kindly telegram which stated,

"YOU HAVE BEEN KIDNAPPED>LEAVE AT ONCE>GET ON THE FIRST TRAIN TO BUENOS AIRES. TELL THEM YOU HAVE A FAMILY EMERGENCY YOU MUST LEAVE>OR TELL THEM NOTHING AT ALL JUST GO GET OUT OF THERE!"

Dear Louis, I'm having a good time here in Argentina there is more snow than New Hampshire and the mountains are bigger, I may never come home at all, well when I run out of money but it's not costing me much at all. And besides I don't like stepmother all that much but I see why you do-big teats!

My grandmother Wolf was very anxious for me and hired two operatives to rescue me, all for a big sum of money of course. They were brothers of the same father and I never learned their names but realized there cover was blown and they were probably executed. Later their father put a hit on me much later.

I was young and naïve not exactly all my fault.

My father visited Paul Valar in Sugar Hill and accused him of hiding Nazis even though he was Swiss and his wife Paula a bronze medalist from Czechoslovakia. They had no idea my father was the US Government at least not at first. The government wanted all those German patriots down in Argentina and Chile to kill communists. Our beloved government was still at war.

LIPSKY

5:12 AM

My own assessment of Josef Lipsky was that he was a traitor.

Of course my father, Louis, reprimanded my lack of understanding and told me quite confidently that Lipsky was a great man.

I didn't meet him through any normal political channels. I was a sixteen year old in 1964. There I was in San Carlos de Bariloche, Argentina through the grace of our Lord who must have deemed it appropriate. I beheld a small man with a mustache in the great base lodge building there where now is a parking lot as it was outdated and soon torn down to accommodate a tremendous ski village like Aspen with magnificent expensive hotels and chair lifts.

There was none of that in 1964 although an eighteen passenger tramway did exist then plus some tiny surface lifts which consisted of a small cable and a contraption one wore as a waist belt that had a hook to attach but was very dangerous indeed as some females with long hair had tangled in the cable and been dragged through the bull wheel screaming to their deaths.

On weekends there was an upper chairlift with a tremendous lift line if it was open and the wind was not blowing hard. Nice powder snow could be found up there on the high mountain ridge four thousand feet above the long Andes Mountain Lake Nahuel Huapi which stretched over thirty miles long almost to the Chilean border.

Perhaps it was a different year altogether maybe 1966 or 1968, those years I also managed to go there though at the disapproval of my father for some reason he had said,

"Don't go there, Bariloche!" He had been quite adamant.

On the ski lift beside me was a young blond girl probably my senior by a year or two who spoke some broken English quite well. She said,

"Oh you are American. We don't see many of your kind here. She was a very excellent skier with blue eyes and a big smile. She told me the Refugio restaurant on the ridge was named for her father, a Pole, who had helped many of the refugees from the war arrived safely in Bariloche. I ascertained the refugees were all Nazis and that her father was a big shot lawyer I should meet so she invited me to dinner at their house where I might meet her younger sister who she implied was not a skier but more my age though darker and shapely which I ascertained meant her teats are big.

So I went to the German looking chalet at the address she gave me arriving there it was already dark and an older woman greeted me, Lipsky's second wife and mother of the darker younger daughter,they were Spaniards and very friendly though the dark daughter soon ran to her room and hid.

At the dinner table was the father not entirely amused by my arrival. He wasn't wearing the big Orthodox mink or sable hat that characterized him as he walked to his business, his law office probably upstairs above a Coffee Shop and Tea House where locals drank and played chess and Dominos.

"American, do you know that the Polish underground surrendered in the Warsaw Ghetto uprising to whom do you suppose?"

"The Russian liberators?" I responded wrongly thinking I knew the answer being young and naive.

"No! No! They surrendered to the Third Reich for honorable citizenship, American!" he insisted.

"That's absurd!" I countered.

"Leave my house immediately, no dinner for you!" He shouted, very relieved to have an excuse to free his dinner table and daughters of me.

Of course I left immediately and hungry and back I went to my hostel with no dinner at all now that everything was closing down in Bariloche, a small hamlet of five thousand people back then. Nowadays it is well over a hundred thousand maybe two as the Mapuche Natives could smell the Swiss baking chocolate so they all came running to the little Swiss now Nazi village to be maids and butlers, waiters and bartenders, bus drivers and snow shovelers.

Lipsky had been the Polish ambassador to Berlin in 1939 when Germany invaded Poland at the beginning of World War II. Luckily he had befriended Goering, second in command to Hitler himself so a spot was reserved for him in the future other than in the gas chambers at Treblinka. Lipsky was given full paid passage to go to Argentina where he would complete the Bar Exam and become an Argentine lawyer specializing in Immigration Law in case Germany should lose the war he would be there to greet the refugee arrivals, possibly even Hitler himself!

In exchange for his good treatment by the Nazis he disclosed to Goering the exact locations of every Jewish settlement in Poland so the inferior sick people could be rounded up quickly and indoctrinated in extermination camps which might even spare a few. Arbeit mach Frei (Work shall free us).

ARGENTINA CANNOT MAKE UP HER MIND, SHE IS FICKLE

In trying to figure out the complicated psyche of the Argentine Republic: After visiting Argentina as a tourist in 1964, 1966, 1968, 1971, 2008, 2009, 2011, 2012, 2013, 2018 and 2019 my very subjective and personal conclusion is: Argentina thinks it lost World War II. It stayed neutral in World War I as well as World War II even though its neighbor Brazil decided to fight with the Allies and sent Brazilian soldiers to the front lines. Argentina has always distrusted its larger neighbor to the north. A brief war between them was responsible for creating buffer states of Paraguay and Uruguay.

The original people of Brazil had emigrated from Africa 19,000 years ago and became the Amazona and Moche peoples as well, culminating perhaps in the Inca Empire.

Argentina or Republic of La Plata was first governed from Lima, Peru but broke away due to its vast distance over the Andes Mountains only to have its governing city Buenos Aires temporarily invaded and occupied by the British Imperial Navy for two years. The Argentines never forgot this insult and distrust all English speaking nations to this day even fighting for the Malvinas Falkland Islands in a war 1982 and losing.

The sentiments of the rich and powerful here have always been with Spain and Italy to a slightly lesser extent. So with Franco ruling Spain after the Spanish Civil War of 1937 and with Mussolini the Fatshist in power in Italy, Argentina was tempted to ally itself with Germany against public opinion here.

It did join the Allies only when Germany was in full retreat.

So the misery of Argentina is like that of a very rich woman in a divorce because she never quite blended in with her in-laws the league of all nations even though she is a very pretty bird indeed she is aloof and detached.

Her biggest cause of failure seems to be her overwhelming agricultural success: she helps feed the world and exports most of her food while importing manufactured goods from everyone else, especially Brazil her rival and increasingly China for shoes and clothes, telephones and computers.

She lives too far from Wall Street to really fathom what is going on and her brokers take advantage of her distance to mismanage her assets. This has led to a national misery and her favorite diamonds have been stolen by international thieves, though she is still young and beautiful, still she is naive and suffers for her infatuations with cavaliers who flatter her immensely but ride off on fast horses to distant villas.

FILL MY HEART, OH GOD (BUS RIDE SANTIAGO TO TEMUCO)

Sun, Aug 20, 2017 9:19 PM

Great thanks to God
Who has given unto me a perfect life with
Many trials and tribulations
Without which I would not know grace
For grace was born out of my despair and humiliation
I cried out to be heard by another
Many friends came and went
But I am left alone in my defeat
Unless I shall cry out to my God, my love
The One who loves me Whose Love I am
Fills my heart with righteousness and joy
Oh how lucky I am to read these words
Because they are from God's love not even my own
It is He who guides my pen, His rod and staff are beside me
How lucky I am that God is still with me
The nations shall all bow down on His day of judgement and
Terrible fury for it is the Lord, so slow to anger
Who is coming to vindicate His People
He shall lift them up out of misery
They did ride among clouds upon the mountaintops
Like David and Saul upon the ridges
He shall scatter the enemies of Israel
Into the ruins of desolate forsaken lands

But God´s people shall have a home
A kingdom with a King
For God is their wall and defense
He never forgets His own

FLYING

Wed, Nov. 11, 7:10 AM

I had the not so enjoyable but somewhat thrilling plane ride while still handcuffed I was begging for them to be removed. I was lowered into my seat in the German Air Force Trainer plane its propeller now loudly turning over it made a hell of a lot of noise then taxied into position and took off. I was still under the influence of sodium pentathol or some other drugs prescribed to me by the man with the mustache, Dr Fritz who had been in the ski troops he claimed at or near Stalingrad. I must have passed out with my eyes rolling back in my head until of course the plane rolled sharply very sharply now we were upside down and that's when I proceeded to vomit all over the canopy above me but now it was below me the plane going into a dive I lost my stomach, so to speak. Of course I hadn't eaten in three days, perhaps a few glasses of water and a few tablespoons of soup probably with drugs in it and those shots they kept giving me probably to keep me sedated.

The plane had some kind of whistle but not quite as loud as a Stuka dive bomber as the Argentines had complained that it startled their cattle chickens livestock and made to many children cry so Rudel was prohibited from dive bombing over the downtown Bariloche as he had once or twice when drunk. He liked to drink but the plate in his head required other drugs prescribed by Mengel some doctor, I didn't quite get the name. Anyway the consumption of alcohol was not recommended and in fact warned against as it might produce some psychological problems such as pronounced repeated hysterical laughter while dive bombing, kidnapping or murdering all of these apparently his specialties. I was a mere sixteen years of age and despite their protests especially Otto with the scar, the big man who was terribly mean and kept slapping me-I kept passing out going unconscious.

"The problem with torturing children," said otto Skorzeny, "Is that they keep passing out, robbing us of all our pleasure!"

I didn't know if all their pleasure would ever cease at all but then a detective and Mrs. Leatherby, the Chilean Ski Team chaperone found me in some motel room where I had been deposited and the detective made my drink nonstop coffee to bring me out of me coma as permanent brain damage had been their objective for me the suspect spy.

Mrs Leatherby came up with her best plan for my getaway by placing a scarf on my head a ribbon bangs and lipstick and yes a dress I was wearing as we were loaded into the boat to cross the big lake to go back to Chile,An old Constable and thirty young boys dressed in Lederhosen and Bavarian attire then approached the dock,

"Vee are looking for that American did you see him? We are too arrest him!" They were looking and I was acting like a poor peasant mapuche maid with my shoulders slumped yes we were soon lake bound despite all their protesting the boat captain insisted he had a schedule to keep. I left Argentina. But in Chile Mrs. Leatherby had a marine stand guard to my room in Puerto Varas then in Santiago she said I must go to Portillo on my own so I took a bus to Los Andes where I met my friends the Syrian Arab family who had heard the rumor some strange men were looking for me and it was Sunday with no train going to Portillo so they recommended I go with their sons up to the Christ statue about a three mile walk uphill as no Nazis would go there. I did. Next day I went to Portillo where ski patrol Schafer was furious and said my father had just arrived by plane and was coming to get me take me home. I had disobeyed orders, I would be court marshaled and stripped of rank, discharged from the Navy.

ROSE

2005

Rose

It's quite sad about Rose

She had no clothes

Very bad clothes if any

But boyfriends she had many.

She lived high on the third floor

Her door I still adore

Though she was very poor,

If she had some she'd be sore

But what was sure

Her heart was pure

While mine still burns

I never did learn

One day she went away

Where she went I will not say

Only that she did not stay

So I pray

Jesus in heaven if you see Rose

You'll love her even if her nose

Is slightly crooked

She is not wicked

Her toes are licorice

Her lips are very nice

Her hips do quite suffice

Her thighs catch my eyes In her bathing suit

The owls in the trees do hoot

At her on the porch

As for the stork

Who comes after we uncorked

Champagne on Lake Champlain

Vous est mon fille

Sirle juvenile

Duncan Cullman

Still you're pretty and I see

You in my dreams

Your skin is cream

De liquor un parfait

De chocolat en May

Sweeter than the smelts in Saguenay

Bay what can I say

For her Rose I did pay

She broke my heart she went away

Perhaps to some new kingdom she did not say

Yet she will play

know In bars her flute so gay

Late into the night

Neath stars so bright

Her teeth so white

Her eyes are lights

She's why I write

This verse tonight

Reverse her fate I'll be her mate

We'll soon eat cake

That I will bake

She'll say she should not

because she could not

Stop eating Swiss cheese

She preferred the holes and her knees

Often separated with the warm breeze

Of hot summer Knights

On cotton sheets white

Then she bought a train

Ticket to Spain

To go see Jane in the pouring rain

During the reign of Franco

She seduced Janko

They left in his car

To park in a Parque neath stars

Her long silken robes

Smoother than adobe

Upon her thighs did flow

Then smoothly rise I know

Perhaps that's why she had to

go Off with him to the dinner show.

They had no dog

They often wore clogs For

her he would dance All day and night

She liked that quite

A lot more than talk To the Balkans

The story goes

If you see Rose

My heart is broken

I lost my token for the subway

I parked my car

I walked quite far

Until I found the strip bar And

there she was while he

Was gone and she Remembered me

I said, "Oh Rose see!"

Then she replied to me,

"My name's Shari!"

So I replied, "I'm hairy Harry!"

Mon Cheri I'll be your fairy

She said I like those too

What will you do to see my tattoo?

I will but first let's go

To the beach in Acapulco Because

You remind me of a man I met from Japan

His name was Stan

He had a plan

And a plane

He flew to Spain to see Jane

There he met Rose

So the story goes

He shot her in the head

Now she's quite dead!

I can't quite believe it I said

I do love Jane too

But I love even more you So to Moore

Duncan Cullman

Dam we flew because we are now

Both cuckoo and in a chalet we stay

All night and day

I still pray

For my Rose who went away

I've turned to God

I boil schrod

I walk the dog

Through morning fog I've grown old

My story told

O faded Rose

WHEN LOVE CAME

When love came into this world

It came from the parents to their children

The children received it but did not know
how to pass it on unless instructed

The love is a constant k, it is the power of the universes

The father has given it to me which came from his parents to him

Our fathers have passed on the love given
by God to Adam in the creation

I receive the love given me from the Father in order to pass it on

In so doing I am protected from evil and temptation
which leads to disease and suffering

The love of the father (and my mother as well) is
in me and if God also therefore is my

Father, then I am His son also

And He is in me and I am therefore included in Him, born again

To be an integral part of God, our Creator, like the angels are as well

Duncan Cullman

Because we are all servants of the boss in line of succession

We are soldiers of the love itself to fight for good

Which is predestined to triumph over evil (like in the Bhagavad Gita)

There is no advancement in the army of God without love

We are called to make friends and keep them because we love them

We are all God's children even if we are atheists
we still can discern what love is

When love came at the Creation it continues to
come and always shall because God lives

forever

So let us be disciples of the greatest of lovers,
God whose love is given for us

That we live in truth and glory all our days with no fear

Until we recover from the illnesses of our bodily lust and overcome

Because we are born to triumph in the battle, our army of good will win

Therefore I ask you to join the army of good
and God to win this very day

Let your lantern be a beacon for those lost upon the sea in despair

Bring them all home to salvation through our Lord, your Father also!

Amen

CONNIE

Constance Hendricks I remember as one of the best of the best people on the planet. She was petite and blonde and not particularly muscular for a ski racer which she was for Oberlin College in Ohio. Born in 1942 to Malvin Jackson Hendricks she was the granddaughter of an Eaton as well making her unknown to me a ninth cousin of Gordi Eaton of Middlebury College and Olympic ski fame as well as a seventh cousin to me but I did not discover this until forty years later. I was eighteen. She was twenty three and preferred Dartmouth men. I was something she entertained because probably my grandfather MacBride in Boston or my granny Darthea MacBride decided it well worth it to hire her to transport me to ski races the winter of 1966.She loved her VW bug and was a lifelong advocate for them. They did get great gas mileage and were easy to push out of snowbanks. We went everywhere on those cold frozen and slushy weekends 1966 as it would rain as well as snow. But the Stowe Cup of 1966 she had an invitation with some rich family and I was not invited so she dumped me off at the homeless shelter although they didn't call it such it was Mother Marie's bunkhouse then and for one dollar you could spend the night although there were no sheets or blankets just burlap covered bunks. My parka sufficed for my blanket. Thank God she arrived during breakfast which was hardtack and coffee. Off we went to race the Stowe Cup slalom: I won and she was sixth she said but maybe ninth in fact. She struggled with her racing but developed an avid crush on a Dartmouth student David Reid from Seattle who would take third in Mt Washington Inferno three years later then skip out at the finish line avoiding his picture being taken maybe back to school to study albeit etc.

The next day was the Stowe Cup downhill and the college coaches were mumbling how a high school kid like me should not be allowed to win and so Earl Morse, future ski coach of Johnson State College in Vermont, a son of Morse Dairy farm in nearby Montpelier skied toward the starting gate at fifteen miles per hour once summoned there and did not stop but skied right through it with considerable momentum and won the race beating me by a full second. I was second place and Connie decided not to compete. We went for Pizza. We stopped for tea. We drove by her father's house on the street corner Hudson, NH. It was an odd little house that stuck out into the roadway. She had a sister Sandra who was a yoga teacher there at Johnson State College. I applied for a scholarship and Earl had me accepted in 1970 but it was learned that my father was rich in New York, hence no scholarship and the tuition was upped from $1300 to $3500 hence I did not attend due to a lack of funds. Connie thought me selfish and self-centered and gave me the ditch for probably David Reid. I hold nothing against her and she is still most dear to my heart.

Perhaps I'll see her in heaven. She died in a car wreck in Washington State 1998.Perhaps she was in a VW bug or Volkswagen something. God bless her soul and Earl Morse as well and all those ski racing Alumni from Johnson State as I see many on Facebook but I do not attend reunions anymore.

WELCOME TO SUGAR HILL, NEW HAMPSHIRE: IF YOU WERE NOT ON CAMERA THEN YOU INDEED ARE NOW! THERE WILL INDEED BE NO MORE SHENANIGANS!

Welcome to Sugar Hill

I first moved to Sugar Hill in 1965 which is now half a century ago to be in fact. So I was no native there but being young, eager, bright eyed and more importantly able bodied I found employment building tennis courts and fixing bicycles and then selling them, and in the farm fields of Sel Hannah where at times I was the only employee. No one else was motivated to pick long rows of potatoes. One day my girlfriend Betsie Alt helped me. One day was enough for her too.

So this is my story of love and adventure in the general region. This being the jet age it is known we do wander around a bit and get lost too. So this is a story about the people I met, the young ladies I dated who were the most beautiful in all my world.

Some of the first people I met there were the Connors brothers Nick and Greg, whose father owned the shoe company in Littleton. So if making shoes had been my lifelong ambition, I could have gone to work right then and there. But shoes were not exactly my thing unless mine wore out. Now we have Walmart for that. Back then we had Marge Libby to remind us.

"Your shoes are worn out and your clothes aren't much better to boot. I guess it's time to go see Joe LaHout at his store:Joe LaHout Store."

I also met the young ski champion Fred Libby whose father Mickey would work his way up from ski patrol to be general manager on the phone with the Governor of New Hampshire. Mickey had been a foot soldier in World War II and was one of the first to cross the bridge at Remagen and invade Nazi Germany. Almost everyone who had crossed that bridge with him then had been killed.

MICKEY LIBBY

When I first had brought my prospective bride to Sugar Hill, Leave Northward to Sugar Hill we had snuck our way past ticket checkers onto the lower lift but climbed by foot the upper half of Cannon Mountain to arrive by surprise at the ski patrol room in the basement of the Summit Cafeteria building to see Mickey Libby. He was not quite so jubilant as I as he had kicked me off Cannon Mountain repeatedly: over the years.

Of all the people on the planet responsible for my winning the American Inferno Ski Race down Mt. Washington's notorious Tuckerman's Ravine aside from my father who deserves most the credit over all the years it was Mickey Libby who pulled all the necessary strings that one day, April 26,1969.

I had been late and slow in my ascent from Hojo's midway up the mountain and thus I had been forced to hunker down between large boulders as the summit was pummeled suddenly by one hundred miles per hour gusts.

Arriving very chilled with slight hypothermia in the summit cafeteria usually only open summer months, I had ingested steaming cups of coffee to revive me. This would never happened if Mickey, father of my high school friend Fred, had not been there to delay the race as head of Cannon Mountain, State of New Hampshire Ski Patrol.

Indeed if Wildcat Mountain, privately owned, had been in charge of the race it would have gone off on time and I would have missed my start, been disqualified.

I never have ever openly thanked Mickey whose wife Marghie had helped me enroll my senior year in Littleton High School, the worst high school in the State of New Hampshire in the best neighborhood in New Hampshire. Of course Marghie was a Hurlburt aunt of Chucky but I didn't know it at the time. I only knew I wanted to go to school where I could skip my late afternoon study halls and hitchhike to Cannon Mountain Ski Area midweek usually arriving about three o'clock giving me fifty nine minutes to ski maybe five or six runs total.

The High School did offer a few comprehensive classes gearing specifically to children coping with the natural surroundings such as...

1. How to hotwire the family car when it's forty below zero so you can come to the warmer school where lunch is free, care of Uncle Sam
2. How to build doghouses, picnic tables, and Adirondack Chairs to sell to the summer tourists.
3. How to fool your parents into thinking you got good grades when in fact you played hooky all year and had gone skiing in a disguise as Charlie Miller,Mickey's assistant was apt to interrogate every Cannoin Mountain midweek skier with,

"Why aren't you in school today?

I also never had the guile to tell Mickey I had been virtually kidnapped two days before that famous ski race as I had a ski race buddy whose sister dated a mobster. Yes you guessed it his sponsorship for ski racing was in fact the mob itself and that explains all the pot he was selling to pay for the gas in the car we were driving everywhere across the country, Jackson Hole, Aspen you name it we had been there.

Anyway my ski buddy nicknamed "The Napper" as he usually took very long snoozes after a reefer at lunchtime. He had been told by "The family" what the mob called itself to give me a very long ride somewhere without a gas stop without any stops and so I found myself now delivered to the Alleghash Wilderness in northern rural backwoods Maine.

This is I suspect because Tyler Palmer whose father worked for the east coast syndicate and was deeply indebted to the mob, was favored to win the race, or indeed there were in fact some favors being done to insure there might be some payback for North Conways' golden boy and brother Terry who was hoped to be runner-up.

So I said to the Man there in that hut near the Canadian border,

"I've got nothing going on at all in my life so why don't I join up with this Family!" He said sign the papers if I'm really serious and they'll front me some pills.

"Okay, I agreed, my bicycle is on top of the Napper's ski rack, you can fill the frame with the goods for delivery. While I use the restroom."

Most unsuspectedly I started biking that evening as the sun set on the snow covered highway. I just kept pedaling and pedaling from logging road to logging road all the way back to North Conway and though I didn't have more than a few bites of food in my rucksack, I did have Richard Nixon's latest arsenal of drugs developed that the United States military would go into battle fear free with LSD!

Of course I hadn't realized that those signed papers were enough to keep me off the US Ski Team forever.

Yet in fact I only had met Cindy Right because of winning that race two days later.

"Oh you won that race and I was watching it up there in the ravine with my father!" was her opening line. I didn't have the heart to tell her quite a lot of things including much of the above.

DANCING WITH ADOLFO THAT DEVIL

My first contact with the main body of the CIA was the antique car show at Oxford Hunt Club which our property faced to the east. It was visible each and every morning from the dining room as well as the kitchen window above the sink as well as the kitchen breakfast nook. I was a ten year old.

They must have all parked their antique cars across the street in that big pasture usually reserved for trotting horses and polo games, horse shows and dog shows. But here the drivers all came at once into my house, the large colonial living room for a conference that I was immediately sent to bed for even though it was still afternoon, I was not to know or repeat anything about that day at all to anyone. However there were some cracks in the floorboards upstairs and I, with my young sensitive ears, could hear everything that was spoken.

There was to be a great conflict, a war, to be fought by the United States against communism and its proponents and there were varying theories where this war would take place. One possibility was that Brazil would be allowed to go communist and another that this war would be in Southeast Asia somewhere or the Philippines but less likely.

John F.Kennedy, a Catholic, was running for president against Richard Nixon who was currently the Vice President under President Eisenhower, a very popular president and former Allied Commander in Europe in the Second World War. Few people expected a Catholic to win but the very charming John F.Kennedy, a PT boat captain in that war did win.

Immediately once in office Kennedy attempted to dismantle the Old Navy (CIA0, the FBI and the Teamsters Union led by Jimmy Hoffa who disappeared into thin air.

President Kennedy heard about the plan for a war in Brazil and decided he would not allow a war between neighboring Catholics. The Pope agreed. So my father was sent to South America in 1959 and I was selected to accompany him in order that he might appear to be a family man on vacation with Anne Wing who would accompany us and be mistaken for my mother perhaps, at least by observant communists who were thought to be everywhere, especially in bad neighborhoods which we avoided.

I don't think Anne Wing was with us the morning we knocked on the door of the Cusco Cathedral to inquire about the presence of a certain priest (Martin Bormann). The Cardinal insisted that the aforesaid had left for Paraguay though he didn't use those exact words specifically. It was soon rumored by high officials that Martin Bormann, Hitler's adjutant general, had died of yellow fever within months of arriving there with Arnold Hundhammer, A Hitler bodyguard he met up with their whose whereabouts now became a mystery as well though it was rumored he was going to Argentina to meet Mengele.

The very bald man with a few traces of blond hair near his ears who advocated for a war in Brazil was the former Stuka pilot, Hans Rudel who had arrived from England with a wife he married there while the guest of RAF pilot Douglass Bader who had lost both legs. Rudel had lost one and still skied with arm crutches attached to mini-skis.

Rudel rode up the ski lift with me in Portillo, Chile and insisted that I come ski race in Bariloche, a very tidy well organized mountain hamlet on a big sparkling lake Nahuel Huapi. My father had given me specific instructions,

"Don't go there!"

Othmar Schneider, the ski school director in Portillo repeated the warning saying,

"I cannot stop you from going but I advise against it as I cannot protect you there. It is the territory of a different German Gautleiter, Otto Skorzeny, but I will tell him you will be under his protection."

"I will have to grow up soon anyway," I retorted very unwisely.

In Bariloche I won the very last ski race of seven, five of which I could not enter as Bud Little in Montana sent me a telegram stating,

YOU HAVE NO PERMISSION TO REPRESENT THE UNITED STATES! YOU HAVE BEEN KIDNAPPED. LEAVE IMMEDIATELY BY TRAIN OR BUS.

Rudel insisted by gun point in the parking lot that I accompany him to a place where a man wants to buy my skis. Of course during the race Arnold Hundhammer and Dr. Mengele tried to snatch away my skis from me but La Escuela Militar de la Montana, the Argentine Ski Team on face value grabbed back the skis for me to complete my second run.

So Rudel took me to the entryway of Hotel Llao-Llao where a man who looked like Adolf Hitler grabbed me by the ear. I said,

"You're dead!" while in the ballroom I could see a grand waltz party with hundreds of people probably German.

He thought that was somewhat amusing and insisted we dance a few steps. I returned to the parking lot for a game of circle jerk, my very first but a lugar struck me on my right shoulder blade almost breaking it. I passed out.

Amen

HOW MUCH DID I REMEMBER

“How much do you remember?” said the Lithuanian nurse to me
in the Boston Sanatorium’ Then she confided to me secretly,
“I am one of them!” She was a Nazi?
It didn’t really matter much at all. I had told my psychiatrist that
I was no longer happy, my childhood had been ruined completely.
He explained that maybe shock treatments would help me. I was
on the verge of suicide and LSD hadn’t yet been invented.
The kind nurse switched the tags on our beds
or maybe it was the other patient?
In any case they led me off down the long corridors to the electric chair,
I protested but not for very long, the current felt warm, very warm.
There was an awful smell stuck inside of me that wouldn’t
go away. It was my burned flesh, my lost brain cells.

BE HAPPY IT'S THE NEW YEAR (OR BE HAPPY FOR THIS NEW DAY, TODAY!)

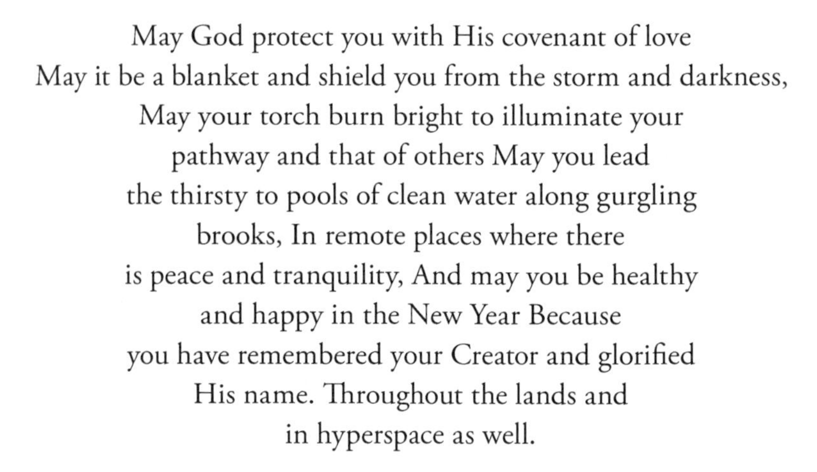

May God protect you with His covenant of love
May it be a blanket and shield you from the storm and darkness,
May your torch burn bright to illuminate your
pathway and that of others May you lead
the thirsty to pools of clean water along gurgling
brooks, In remote places where there
is peace and tranquility, And may you be healthy
and happy in the New Year Because
you have remembered your Creator and glorified
His name. Throughout the lands and
in hyperspace as well.

Amen

THE KARAOKE CROONER

There was a dejected forlorn man who nevertheless was humble and contrite soft spoken and not vicious and he was down in the dumps. His wife had left him because he didn't have a job. He lost his car and house to the bank because he could not make payments. He still had $79 so he went to Walmart and bought a bicycle and took his only broom and went on the sidewalks sweeping them for tips from shopkeepers who decided that he could wash their windows and mop their floors as well. So his life began looking up. At night he studied at church in a bible class about Job.

Job had lost everything. Even his dog probably and the cat too. He entreated the Lord

Please Lord, make me well give me back my health and my faith more or less.

Job was lacking faith and possibly love. Job lived long before Jesus was even born so there was no one to raise him from the dead like Lazarus was raised by Jesus. He would have to crawl out of his own open grave he had dug for himself somehow more or less.

So the man decided to be like Job and ask God for forgiveness for his sins which are far too numerous for ten novels. The wind shifted direction and the morbid stifling smog lifted out of his life. He became a brand new man in a brand sparkling shiny new environment just as though he had been born anew.

The old troublesome memories passed out of his terrible dreams and now there was hope and salvation and joy. He began to sing in the choir at church and at karaoke. His voice wasn't very good and some people's ears were bothered.

But this didn't bother him at all because he was happy and many flocked to him to share his happiness as though it were a contagious antibiotic.

BUTTERFLY

He was only a man

In fact less than a man

Forsaken by his former friends

With no cell phone and no book of addresses

But God was willing

To change him:to mold him

To raise him up out of the dust

Onto a high green mountain

From the summit he beheld

A Distant Kingdom

The one perhaps his ancestors had migrated from?

And there in the distance too

A castle with ivy grown upon its ancient walls

And far above its many moats

A young green Prince was gazing back at him-

Why it was himself indeed!

It was the man he would somehow become?

But change was necessary

He would have to revolt or molt

Out of his old mold and form

Like a moth worm he would need

To sprout some wings and become

A butterfly.

And so one Day he flew indeed He

flew away from his former self Just

a worm he had been

But now with his butterfly wings he soared

Into that distant land

Which is the land we all came from

It is the Promised Land

For God has promised us that

We may all yet be reborn as new creatures

And leave our earthly selves behind,

Our earthly instincts, our greed and selfishness, envy and lust

We will no longer need in our new Home,

Heaven itself to which we must all return,

Because the earth is not our true home.

Our home is with God in Heaven

Out of whose bosom we were all born

Into this forsaken disappointing world of failure and doom.

Surely we have our brief successes

Like an athlete in the Olympics we strive,

But we must realize who we are

That we are indeed the Children of the Living God.

So sleep peacefully and know

It is God alone whose Love does radiate upon the earth.

There is really no other love because the human love is illusory just temporary

As are the seasons of the year

But the Love of our God is eternal and forever.

So rest in peace, remain calm

Do not be overcome by the anxiety in this world

For just as this world shall slowly fade,its anxiety will fade with it

There will just be the songs of all those Angels,

The Ones that filled your mothers ears when you were born

When your eyes finally opened to the new life

So shall it be

Forever

THE MONASTIC LIFE AT ST. BERNARD'S MONASTERY SKI AREA

The Monastery St. Bernard

After exploring south and west in the land of more sun and higher mountains I purchased for two thousand nine hundred ninety nine dollars a patented mining claim entitled Bastile at eleven thousand eight hundred fifty feet altitude, roughly twice the altitude of Mt Washington, New Hampshire; and thereupon after selling my original one acre of land in Twin Mountain, New Hampshire in order to complete the sale with a five thousand mile drive in an orange Datsun hallucinating most of the way just from exhaustion, I hence force began to build a monstrous ten by ten foot cabin with some Ohio hitchhikers I had picked up on the way west: most notably Ken Saffranski who insisted on picking up his girlfriend Dianne Stauder who was pleased with herself to find a ride in any direction after having flunked out of Ohio State her sophomore year due to excessive drinking drugs and wild sex orgies. She proceeded to be so happy she insisted on doing both of us and I being sloppy seconds managed to bring her to an unrivaled climax thereupon she became my girlfriend for almost two years.

I knew Mynx might not be too thrilled about my new companion as Mynx had been up there first to the "monastery" we called it. But Mynx was preoccupied in distant adventures with her Daddy sailing the Atlantic.

Hank Dane and later his girlfriend Michelle Spanos would come visit from Sugar Hill and Indian Head Resort in Franconia Notch. Then Safransky brought his college mate Gus Campagna who found in a bar some Nick Nohava whose last name was an alias as Indiana wanted him but he couldn't go back there! Like the song definitely.

We would drive to town, buy rice, potatoes bullets and beer more beer. The monks seemed to have a passion more for beer and less for brewing wine which was too time consuming. We were so busy playing croquet, horseshoes, skiing on summer snow and inviting every character we could find in Silverton and nationwide to come visit eleven thousand nine hundred feet overnight then climb the grassy ridge to Bonita Peak thirteen thousand two hundred feet. Mynx saved my life in a rainstorm on the far side of the mountain where we had gone on a ski adventure scantily clad in tee shirts when she produced out of a plastic mini-jar three matches of which the third was successful in starting a bonfire. But Mynx was history now. New adventurers arrived from France with indescribable expressions on their faces as they had expected a full hostel with running water.

"Oh we run on over there to the stream for our water!" explained Gus to the awestruck travelers who replied,

"This is not a hostel how did you get a license, in France it is very difficult?"

"Well we are in the process of building the hostel" I pointed to the site seventy yards distant where our fourth building was under construction.

Luckily the Frenchmen and their woman had brought some acid LSD and then there was a nonstop party into the next day so they had fun but departed and we lost our license oh well.

Nick and Gus went to work for Mrs. Stone a hairdresser from Manhattan who bought a Mountaintop of mining claims on the advice of her distant fortune teller who told her to dig straight down into the center of the earth and find rare gems. She had propane heat in her luxurious abode at thirteen thousand four hundred feet while Nick and Gus claimed they shivered sleeping in some kind of cave up there. The bulldozer driver lost his life maintain her road while her husband was very understanding as it was all her money anyway.... Nick and Gus came back to the Monastery after she failed to pay them, another Silverton, Colorado mining story.

So we rescued Phyllis a telephone operator in Grand Junction from her job she hated anyway. She was struggling with her tendency toward alcoholism but at the Monastery alcohol was the alleviant to boredom so she fell off the wagon then moved into town with an Indian selling turquoise then joined a religious cult found God and moved to Texas.

So Nick and Gus went with my good friend from North Conway Jimmy Thompson to Taos where they learned the Hemp farming business and soon produced a few tons for distribution. Thereupon Gus remembered his religious commitments to the Monastery and envisioned God Jesus who told him to throw his portion of the righteous weed into the Rio Grande River which He did and so was saved. Of course Nick flipped out grabbed what he could and departed for the drug trade never to be seen again except perhaps by Jesus Himself perhaps at the Gate.

Dianne too found a higher calling and flew away on a jet plane to Ireland where she fell in love married had two children and proceeded to love mostly "Men of the Sea". At least Gus is my distant friend on Facebook to this day and he is in contact with her and her sister who after using my ski poles left them at the ski area. Jimmy Thompson told me all his war stories so I wrote them down, his hiding under a blasted tree as his position was overrun by North Vietnamese Regulars. He had smoked a lot of the righteous weed and was suffering some paranoia with his post-traumatic stress. Poor baby. Yes we all are poor babies' way down deep inside like Led Zeppelin the song.

The Monastery was sold to an aspiring monk from Telluride for fifteen thousand dollars as unfortunately we had all grown up and moved elsewhere. Jesus, I am sure, follows us everywhere still I hope-

MY DEBUT AS A PITCHER (A NIGHTMARE?)

My debut as a baseball pitcher was eventful and out of the ordinary.

I was brought in from shortstop and instructed just to do my best by my coach who handed me the ball. I was eleven years old. I fired simultaneous strikes over the plate though not at any high velocity.

"Ball, ball, ball!" cried out the umpire.

One of my buddies ran over to me and explained that they the adults were all drunk and messing with us, to just keep pitching despite the obvious carnage and the twelve runs I walked over home plate. I was an oversensitive kid and it was mind boggling that our own coach was permitting this abuse.

My teammates reported this to their parents and the coach and umpire were reprimanded if not fired, but this left an irreversible effect on me. I would never pitch again until sixty four years old in a softball game. It seems destiny was steering me away from baseball toward other sports. Strange it is how our lives our shaped and molded. We are told God is in control and has given us our present situation. God gave us the world wars and the holocaust and the Bataan death march, all of these to strengthen us or just plain annihilate us. I have struggled with this because God wants us to be thankful and praise His Deliverance so if we die we are delivered to be His angels in heaven? GINA

GINA, MY LOVE

Thu, Apr. 26, 2018 6:25PM

In the morning you are here to great my new day

Like the sun warming my every shivering appendage like a kiss to

connect me to the memory of my mother Who first brought me into

this world To know of your love.

Father,I learned to love you too from your love

You were there to keep all our love from spoiling into passion and temper

You were like the cold blue sky

Ever constant ever deep like eternity

This eternal love because our mother earth keeps on spinning

Round and round like your arms wrapped all around me and your legs

To support the foundation of us we are family

Even dogs and cats with our many babies

Fish and flying things,birds singing in the trees now sprouting

Duncan Cullman

Light green budding like our love. When I first

saw your face

We were both married to other unfaithfuls

Never imagining that one day we might yet discover in each other

True and lasting love,it is like a songbird singing

Or like a soft warm breeze, And so I kissed you or No,you kissed me.

How did this happen?

From out of nowhere our grand collision in space, We were just

meant to be In love

Atop whitest mountain peaks,skiing, snowboarding and snow shoeing

Singing our song and dancing our dance

Of life and love

For they are one and we

Are the inheritors of the Truth

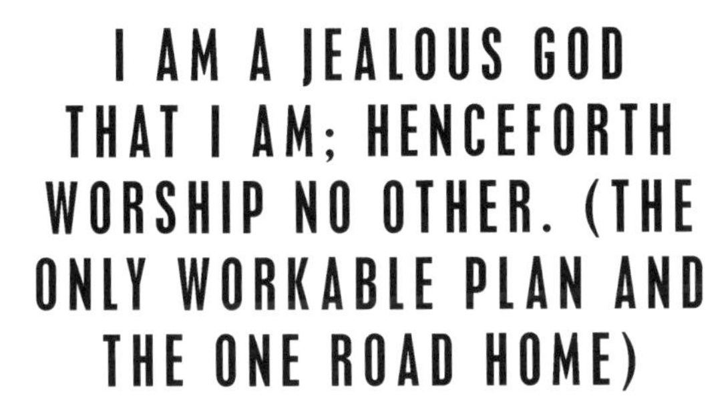

I AM A JEALOUS GOD THAT I AM; HENCEFORTH WORSHIP NO OTHER. (THE ONLY WORKABLE PLAN AND THE ONE ROAD HOME)

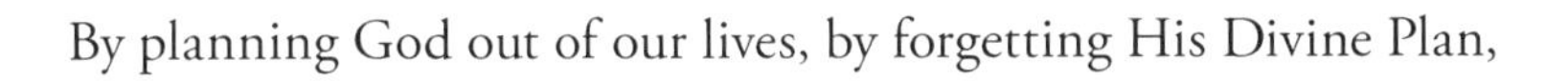

By planning God out of our lives, by forgetting His Divine Plan,

we have opened up that infamous can of worms!

Unhappiness, despair, disappointment, integrated as a result of myriads of illnesses

We are not only fulfilled and made whole by bringing God back into our lives...

we exist in God's great plan in infinity

There is no separate path, because we are on it, for it is the one beneath our feet

Smooth or rocky depending on, for instance,

whether we accept that Jesus Christ is our Lord and Savior who died for our sins

that our have eternal life through Him is our very own being

Other options seem to present themselves that are never excluded, unless we realize;

actualize; and react except to only one apparent path appearing within the truly blessed

toward our living God solely, otherwise allowing for a flaming sea of destruction

Your personal relationship with your living God is your own knowledge of where you stand

If perchance he is a god of death in which case there is no hope or no such thing at all

THE BURGLAR

So the kingdom of heaven is like a thirty five year old burglar

Who breaks into a large mansión with ninety nine rooms

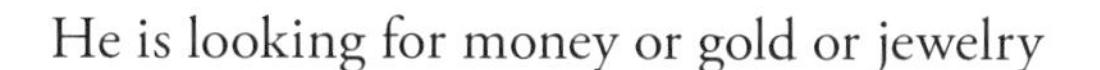

He is looking for money or gold or jewelry

He cases the entire house, room by room

But all the rooms are empty except for some beds sheets and blankets

So he gets very hungry wandering around ninety rooms and goes to the kitchen

Opens the refrigerator and there is a carton of milk and

A large chocolate birthday cake with thirty candles

So he sets it on the dining room table and lights the candles

Then makes a wish that he won't be caught and blows out the candles

Eats the entire cake and drinks the entire half gallon of milk

When lo and behold there is a loud knocking on the door

So he turns off the lights and crawls behind the living room sofá.

Finally he hears the key turning the latch of the front door which is then opened

And Santa Claus enters the house with several packages turning on all the lights

He places them all under the Christmas tree which he plugs in and shouts aloud,

Merry Christmas to you, distant traveler, and welcome home.

The burglar can't control his joy and rips a very loud stinky fart!

But Santa Claus just ignores this because he forgot the ninety eight other Chocolate cakes

and gallons of milk so he races back to the bakery for them Because ninety eight more

burglars are on their way

Imagining they need gold and jewelry and cash

But god knows of their needs better than they do themselves.

ANA, LA SANTA

Sun, Oct. 4, 2015, 9:42 AM

Dear Ana,

Your cousin the cook was outside your restaurant on the sidewalk shaking her ass in a flowery mini-skirt trying to attract Colombian passersby into your Mexican restaurant at a time when Mexican drug wars were headline news, bodies in piles.

She definitely caught my attention her wild brown playful eyes and the attention of a young couple so we entered and ordered the big burrito.

Then you showed up from the bank where your loan officer was nervous.

Then your daughter and son both appeared from school somewhere nearby there in Normandie,a barrio in greater Bogota home of eight million people spread out quite distantly so there are a lot of parks and trees everywhere in the Anti-plano,a high mountain valley between ridges of twelve thousand foot forested peaks the city lies at about nine thousand feet.

Your son realizing you were talking to a North American tourist wanted to ask me if I liked football (as that is what they call soccer) and I replied,

"Yes, Messi the Argentine is very good and diego Forlan,the Uruguayan. Neymar and Ronaldino the Brazilians are also very good."

Your daughter wanted to know where I came from and I responded, "Boston, Massachusetts in Estados Unidos but north in the countryside near the border with Canada."

She didn't know where that was exactly but it satisfied her curiosity for the moment to know such a place might exist but it was so far distant that I might as well have come from the moon itself.

In Colombia they are quite swarthy men much more so than Peru which is more Indian Quechua, Inca,Moche!

I, not being swarthy and not dressed in a dinner jacket and tie with pointed alligator shoes didn't quite fit her equation of Colombian normalcy.

Both your children are well dressed and smart as whips which is what you had wanted for yourself as well as you were born up farther north in a similar mountain valley no North Americans have ever visited overnight and it's not in our atlas map of Colombia: there are thousands of such villages in Colombia not so in Peru which is overrun by New Yorkers as well as everyone else even Europeans.

In Colombia the American tourists are mostly in the larger cities near police or with guides not venturing too far into the unknown which is everywhere Colombian except for the Colombians themselves descended from the Spanish Conquistadors twenty generations ago so they each and everyone knows every square inch at least where their ancestors had trod.

Every time I come to Colombia thereafter I keep visiting you and your growing children who are yes bigger and taller,more grown up now they are ready to attend the university.

While you,although separated for ten years,refuse to file for a divorce as it would be too expensive and you insist you can't go through it all a second time your nerves worn a little thin perhaps.

Colombia is a Catholic country and the ant-iplano is very conservative,not like the coastal regions more known for salsa and African drums. So divorce is easier with a pistol or arsenic or by running away to Bolivia or Ecuador but that is not so easy either.

We have all been caught up in the trap of who we have become all these formative years into later adulthood so we are afraid to venture into the unknown like a gringo tourist in a remote Colombian jungle.

But this is true for the mass of humanity, aging brings on conservatism.

So the years pass by and I am on my computer surfing the web for yet another cheap ticket to Bogota or Asuncion with a stop in Bogota, or for a ticket from Bogota to the Andes where I can ski for a week.

I drive my car every morning to the same breakfast Café to be served by the same smiling waitress wondering where I am going this year to escape!

Every night all summer long I drive to the same softball field and see my teammates who ask me if I'm going on another South American adventure.

"Well",I answer," The local women want nothing to do with me and I don't indulge with prostitutes anywhere,the foreign women are much more interesting and they think I am perhaps from Mars.

I try not to disappoint them. I tell them all about baseball which they have only seen on television but never played. And the vast majority of South Americans have never skied except for a few rich: though some have gone to the Andes and made snowballs after riding a chairlift in rented ski parkas and snow pants and snow boots.

The time goes by, the minutes into hours and weeks into years, and I see a message from Ana on Facebook from Ana.

"Is it true that you are coming to Bogota next month? It will be so good to see you! We can go to coffee someplace nearby...

The children will want to see you but they have children of their own who have heard you are from Mars and will land in your spaceship near the Airport.

O children always love a good story, the world has not changed one iota and neither has Ana!

Earthling, Mother of God, Blessed Virgin daughter of God and kindness and all that is best and good, sweet Ana.

ST. LYNDA AND ST. BRIAN

Sam decided to go hunting again and grabbing three guns promptly loaded them and headed to the bar for a Sam Adams beer of his ancestor Samuel Adams and the bartender Gwen bought ate up his family history and nine months later she gave birth to Samuel Junior.

So Gwen stayed home and changed diapers while Sam went hunting every day before work, after work and during the lunch hour. "Bang! Bang! Bang!"

Sam would bring them home throw them all at his wife and young son and say,

"Skin these,pluck these and then cook these!"

Then Sam decided to go hunting in the Vermont woods near Ryegate and he looked up into a tree thinking perhaps it was a big black bear up there but no it was Brian Pendleton the youngest of twelve children born on Loch Lyndon Farm to his Pendleton parents heirs of Pendleton fuzzy wool company, world renowned!

Brian's father liked to make an example of Brian flogging him daily in order to keep the other eleven children in line. So the traumatized boy who brain was then stymied by this never quite matured into an adult though his body grew and grew hairier like a big wolf at first but eventually he received his well-deserved nickname from close friends,

"The bear!" they called him.

I first met Brian I had thought when Craig took me over to the "Gone With The

Wind" Pendleton mansion with pillars and a waterfall fountain saying to me,

"You gotta meet this guy!" Actually I had almost met him once before at age eleven on Lyndon Outing Club Ski Hill where there was a ski race for us kids. Our parents drank from a flask in the parking lot while we all frolicked to and fro, jumping over the stone wall on our skis.

Brian had piercing black eyes that emitted from a full black beard: this made him look like across between Che Guevara, Karl Marx and Charles Manson the murderer also. I really didn't see much of Brian until I wanted to steal his very pretty new girlfriend everyone was talking about, Lynda Ollssen who had moved in with him to enjoy his newly inherited riches, a trust fund of almost a half million dollars. Unfortunately for her he had already spent most of it but still had the big mansion

He had by now crashed two new cars and received two Driving under the Influence charges. The family yacht in Bean Pond also was missing having sunk in a wild party with all his newfound alcoholic friends.

Plus he had dated some fraudulent females, wined and dined them and then passed out waiting for them when they all went to the ladies room but snuck out the window.

So Lynda really came to his rescue but was unfortunately too late to save his fortune which he had squandered. Her father was in fact Colonel Marvin Olssen of the United States Air Force and behind Lynda's home there was indeed a three thousand foot mountain in Vermont which housed North American Defense NORAD and SAC Strategic Air Command. Minuteman missiles were linked to the position and organized to be fired at command.

We somehow being young stupid boys failed to grasp the significance of all that was too slowly becoming obvious: that anyone knocking up Lynda would probably be set for life as Marvin was not in fact Dwight Eisenhower but almost the equivalent.

Being an idiot I thought I was supposed to go to work every day picking rocks behind the Town of Sheffield road grader on those muddy back roads in Vermont called Class Three: when for a fact I was dating Marvin Olsen's daughter a freelance wandering flower child she wanted to take me hiking, swimming and straight to Paradise on Earth, Shangri-La but I had been too stupid. Brian failed miserably too even though he had no visible job he didn't quite have the instinct to make her Day-give her a child!

So along came a guy with a chainsaw from the backwoods of Westmore, he started the noisy smoky thing up, pointed it at her as she ran into the closet and their daughter Leeah was born nine months later and Marvin was thrilled with a granddaughter to add to one grandson already, Robert the chef. Someone had got lucky several years before and knocked Lynda up but nothing became of that relationship and the grandparents Marvin and Minnie were raising the child because Lynda preferred Grateful Dead concerts and blowing grass and dropping acid at least all her young carefree adult days because why not do all that because Daddy is doing very well.

So Marvin decided to place Lynda in a rental apartment in Lyndonville which is a town where three rivers converge creating the appearance of maybe a fifty year flood plain.

Sure enough come spring it began to rain, rain and rain some more. The river rose ten feet over its flood level and so Lynda was floating around her living room in a big Rubber Ducky made for the Beach while breastfeeding Leeah who was crying as the lights went out. The water subsided in forty eight hours and Lynda went to work where her father was a foreman in a factory for forty more years in a row. This drove her to drink but luckily she found Garth a high school basketball star where she had attended so they were happy as he mowed lawns with a large lawnmower bought probably with Marvin's good credit and he at least helped her by barbecuing in the backyard daily. They ate on disposable paper plates and soon had fifty goats to drive back the woods a bit.

Fred Franklin had long disappeared moving back into his father's house because his Father was dying, he now decided to marry his stepmother which made them both happy. I did see him once as he was trying to sell a trailer in the middle of nowhere near Newark Pond. Unless someone tells you about these places you would not be able to find them on your own because there are no roadmaps to these places in Vermont where the Green Mountain Boys had first ganged up to shoot New York tax collectors then turned their wrath on the British Army defeating them at Saratoga, N.Y. in the Revolutionary War.

Leeah began roller-skating in her basement with my roller-skates. So I bought her some of her own and she is a Roller Derby Queen down in Jersey near where she goes to school, Manhattan the Big Apple!

Upon graduating from Columbia University, she decided to move back to Vermont and become, well can you guess? A hippy in her mother's shadow! Well first she sold tires but now she sells grapefruits and watermelons at Littleton Farmers Market and Saint Johnsbury Farmers Market.

Meanwhile Marvin cutting grass in his backyard on a very large mower on a slight embankment rolled it over on top of himself. He was eighty years old by now and me and Brian went to the funeral and saw Lynda, Leeah and Garth and Fred was there too. Very sad.

Lynda's mother had hated me at first sight likewise to all mothers on the planet they seemed to have a lot in common. Robert had become a cook in Burlington but now that both grandparents had died he moved back locally into their house and became a "Keeper" what Brian calls those who are in charge of groups of mentally disabled persons attended for instance the free daily luncheon in St. Johnsbury at a different church each different day, seven days a week there as Vermont has become a sort of welfare state.

Brian and I applied for the medical marijuana program but were turned down due to the fact we do not suffer terminal illness. Whose subterranean basements of those St Johnsbury churches one can find people that belong in a Charles Dickens novel. They have the appearance of having been bombed out in London by the Luftwaffe in 1941 during the London Blitz, Battle of London!

Of all my friends only Brian and I are regular attendees of these morbid eerie looking affairs but quite feeling as there are usually several deserts.

I reasoned perhaps that I indeed needed a career and so imagined myself to be Duncan Heinz, a food taster of various Dinner Bells. Ring. Ring. Ring. Are you hungry enough to come see all the wretched starving masses?

My previous career of figure skating had suddenly ended age ten when I had fallen through the ice on Bean Pond.

I am going to the Dinner Bell tomorrow at South Church and I have some Blondie rap music to play while I watch all the freaks there as I have become one myself indeed.

ST. BUTTONS

Fri, Oct 2, 2015, 5:59 PM

I had managed to steal one of Brian's girlfriends Lynda and he was not terribly happy about it as she had been with him over nine months. So he had to find another and due to his depleted resources he needed to find one with income, namely a job yet didn't have one except for Christmas Trees which lasted about two months cutting down the trees and tying them in bundles and submerging them in a cold lake plus planting new trees to replace those harvested. Usually he was able also to work around three weeks at Christmas for the United States Post Office shipping and handling but mostly they used him for handling mostly the very heaviest packages as his temperament was not the best working alongside other people; but the same could be said about me as well.

None of his jobs however deterred him from attending every Dinner Bell, Ring! Ring! Free Meal whenever possible between jobs all too few and far between, the same thing could be said for me as I became likewise an enthusiastic Dinner Bell, Ring! Ring! Attendee likewise.

Occasionally in Vermont which is known for being a little left of center in its politics, various employed attractive successful women even college teachers would attend these free Ring! Ring! Dinner Bell Dinners and save a buck plus become nourished to boot.

"Buttons" as Brian nicknamed her after becoming acquainted with her actually had a name Denine Spivak and she was recently divorced from a New York Attorney named Talbot(I would imagine)Spivak. Plus she had a small child Asha, which might even be a Jewish name, I do not know, except that Talbot was referred to as of being that persuasion.

Denine taught yoga and creative writing at Craftsbury College which catered to the very rich who needed special attention they might afford or more likely their rich parents might pay for in beautiful not too far from New York or Boston, Vermont where classes were limited to less than twenty students in a magical setting such as "Moonlight in Vermont" the song describes.

So the well-mannered Brian, his father having beaten manners into him and his siblings as was a very tough dairy farmer rising up at three o'clock every morning to attend his "Girls" as he called his Dairy cows, had exactly the background nostalgia Denine was magically attracted to. And as Brian spent days in his deer stand occasionally bagging a tasty young buck or too, Denine enjoyed the freshly killed tasty seemingly endless gourmet venison dinners.

But because she was an avid Buddhist attending various Buddhist meditations and the

like as soon as Brian had dozed off one evening she arose and managed to break into my room, the door of which was blocked to try to avert such an occurrence but there I was lying in my underwear up on my kickstand as they call that in New England as I must have been dreaming of females and had a righteous Woody to boot. In New England terminology a "Woody" is something as hard as wood that won't soften for a very long time and it is given credit by many women in retrospect as causation for multiple offspring and progeny!

In fact Bodie's father even had "Woody" as his nickname for Woodson which is actually about the equivalent.

Brian, having woken up in the early morning hours and noticing his precious Denine had escaped to double her sexual appetite immediately grabbed his bow and arrows and ventured onto the front lawn where Denine soon arrived smoking a cigarette with a happy smile as well as me with a shit eating grin.

Aiming his bow at ninety degrees straight up into the sky he quickly released seven

arrows to our absolute horror as we indeed that what goes up must come down. Sure enough in those few seconds which seemed like an eternity as we expected perhaps to enter Eternity very abruptly, Twang, twang. Twang. Twang. The arrows landed in the roof five feet away, in the lawn three feet away in the driveway ten feet away! I had suddenly been brought back into the middle Ages in which Brian himself seemed to be living into the twenty first century.

Denine was not deterred one bit and her voracious sexual appetite made her indeed a legend even in the Court Report of St. Johnsbury which ultimately cost her the teaching job with Craftsbury College but then she had taken another part time job with nearby Goddard College at least for a while until her nocturnal and noonday activities surfaced.

She particularly enjoyed displaying her nakedness and very good figure in Dairy Barns, horse barns and sheds to usually married farmers who enjoyed partaking in her antics. Brian meanwhile shot more arrows into the sky one landing between his feet somehow, a very close call.

Chucky Herbert then said to me,

"Confess then that you had sex with the Creature (he called her)!" laughing.

I confess I was overcome by love and am saddened by the news of her death on ancestry.com. It seems Talbot died the same recent year. They are missed.

49 BUICK ROADSTER

Thu, Sep 24, 2015, 9:45 PM

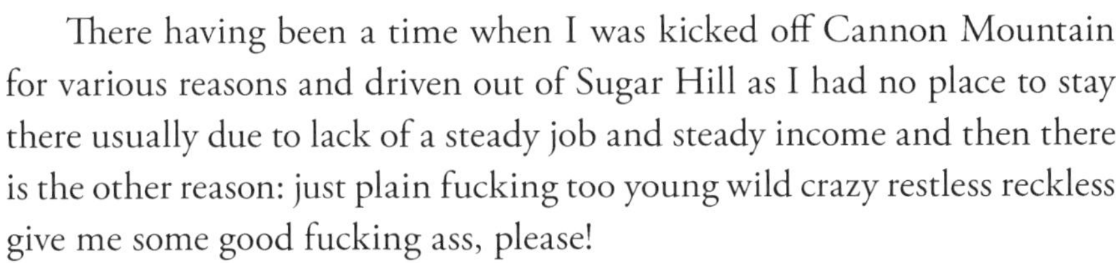

There having been a time when I was kicked off Cannon Mountain for various reasons and driven out of Sugar Hill as I had no place to stay there usually due to lack of a steady job and steady income and then there is the other reason: just plain fucking too young wild crazy restless reckless give me some good fucking ass, please!

I had moved over to North Conway and discovered while over there that a lot of other people my own age were also living in the streets, paying no rent, dropping acid smoking weed, and sometimes even selling drugs to get enough money to buy a $250 car like my Buick Roadster that had no title because the owner wanted it driven a bit then returned.

So at least we had a car to live in. maybe it was a 1948 Buick Roadster but we had a registration for it anyways as skipper Stevens of Freedom, New Hampshire on the Maine border that's why you haven't heard of that town, yes Skipper knew the owner but wanted me to register it as I had a job at Attitash dynamiting ledge for the construction of ski lift towers for Thaddeus Thorne, war hero from the Pacific Arena in the War against Japan WWII. Yes Thaddeus had good credit as he had found a millionaire partner and he himself an army engineer plus an engineering degree. He had a family and five beautiful daughters including one I had been taking to some Drive-In movies and of course we weren't there to watch movies at all in her station wagon with a mattress in back. Her name was September and when she smiled, which was almost always, she looked just like Marilyn Monroe.

Unfortunately on one date with her I encountered a jealous local youth who just wanted to beat my brains out for no rhyme or reason but just to illustrate that he had taken boxing lessons and was on the high school wrestling team: Fred Hayley.

So because I lost the fight probably due to my unhealthy lifestyle living in a car etc, September ditched me thinking I might be on heroin or something. Hashish maybe heroin no, I'd heard that was a no-no drug you would be gone for life doing that you'd be just a loser at everything.

So there I was living in my car and we all decided to drop acid and go see the new French Box Hit, Grand Prix, a car racing movie!

"Gentlemen, start your engines! Rmmm Rmmm!"

In the final scene in order to win the comeback race the world's greatest ever driver goes to make a pass when the wheels of the two cars interlock and all the hub bolts are sheared off so a wheel comes loose and our hero's car careens off the track into a tree. He dies!

OMG. I hadn't been expecting this and the curtain comes down and I am still glued to my seat unable to move as though it's a formula one race seat in the lead car:am I dead?

My friends are snapping fingers in my face, the theater ushers are there wanting me to leave. My friends help me to me feet explaining to the ushers,

"Oh, he's just high on acid, ha,ha,ha,ha!"

So we crawl into the roadster parked across the street in an alley and it won't start. Dead battery, no lights. It begins to snow, the first snow of the season late fall.

The girl on my lap is a local farm girl. Her parents being farmers had no money to fix her very large buck teeth. She wears giant glasses that are now steaming up inside the car where our every breath can be seen as it is quite cold out now. I have always loved her and always watched her and always thought to myself,

"What a nice girl, the kind to marry, not great looking but genial and friendly and warm"

Now I am pulling her pants down in the cold car cramped with five other people trying to sleep some snoring. I am hard and she wants me.

There is nothing to do to warm us up better than to screw her. She has no perfume and no deodorant neither do I so it's quite an animalistic ritual having been done I pulled out like an idiot when the best thing for us both would have been Immaculate Conception: God at work trying to build families upon the Earth, His Dominion. I guess we were not quite ready for that. I guess we figured for the immediate foreseeable future we had no homes to live in, only an occasional car, an occasional tent!

We are like stray dogs poor and undernourished in the streets. We cannot proliferate. We cannot proliferate. Doesn't God loves us at all? We are all his children.

NITA JOVENCITA

Fri, Aug 10, 2018 8:52 PM

La Nita jovencita Bonita

Once upon a time in a country shaped like a spaghetti called Chile, A land in South America which is a continent the southernmost

Part is a triangle and is called Patagonia because the wind blows hard out of the west from the Pacific Ocean and southerly at times from the frozen continent of Antárctica

In a small town called Pucon,a tiny hamlet,

Into which a mother dog gave birth to her puppies in the house of Carlos and his wife Tapiadora. There were now born there five puppies and they were very tiny so the mother dog licked them all to make them cleanñand of course she nursed them all.

After ten weeks the puppies grew to be big fat happy puppies and so people came to see them if they might be ready for adoption to go to new homes where families would love them. All of the puppies found homes but one because she was nervous and high strung and seemed full energy chewing up everything in sight. Her name was Linda or at least Carlos called her that because she was good looking and she wandered around a lot like a Beagle, perhaps she had inherited some Beagle genes from somewhere?

Carlos' wife Tapiadoria chased Linda all around the house and out the door screaming at the little Linda who seemed to pee everywhere and not be housebroken. Now she was out in the streets where cars could run her over and bigger dogs could bite her. She was afraid to go home because Tapiadora had hit her with the mop. So she wandered with the big dogs. In Latin America there is no leash law still so animals can run free which many do all day then they go home at night to their owners who let them inside to sleep on a dog bed perhaps in an entryway or a garage or a mudroom. But Linda had no home and so she wandered around the town like a Beagle meeting everyone. There were some people who were homeless like her, an old man Agostino and his wife Abuelita. Also there were some other homeless dogs like Noruegita and Leonardo,Leon de los Calles and Nieve,Amarillo y Blondie y Princesa Negra.

Linda came to the Adventure Center tienda every day to see Carlos who remembered her and gave her the last uneaten bits of his lunch. He felt sorry for her that Tapiadora, his wife, had evicted her for spontaneous peeing everywhere. The adventure Center was a meeting point for tourists who wanted transportation to the snow on Volcano Rukapillan which is a fiery volcano like Pompeii that rises two thousand four hundred meters above Pucon. In 1985 just decades ago it exploded with rocks and lava which raced down its mountainside destroying the ski area. After seventeen years of dormancy the new owners decided to rebuild the ski area in a new place where lava might not reach in any subsequent eruptions…

Luckily for Linda a tourist came to town again, one that had fed her some hotdogs the year before. She remembered him and he remembered her though he had only seen her twice the year before. Now he spotted her on the sidewalk every day and brought her leftovers from his breakfast wherever he found her sleeping in the warm sunshine among grass and flowers in the median of Main Street among flowers. Homeless dogs are very tired from fighting with other dogs all night long over scraps of garbage and whatever they can find to eat which isn't much at all.

"Jovencito "",said the tourist she remembered not realizing she was a female he called her a young thing. So her name eventually could have been shortened to Cita but became" Nita Jovencita Bonita ` ``.The tourist whose nickname soon became Ducon Pucon loved her very much and it was reciprocal love, though he soon left for Argentina for two weeks he worried about her in dreams and everyday skiing and riding the chairlifts of cerro Catedral. So he returned to find her sleeping in the main street median garden between the two lanes in a bed of roses. She was such a pretty dog too.

Carlos did his best to encourage Ducon to adopt the very Linda pretty Nita jovencita and a lady in the tourist agency next door named Amanda told Ducon that her best friend was a veterinarian named Claudia Mascaballos who she called on the telephone and Claudia told her and Ducon that Chile would give free puppy shots to Nita for any foreigner who might want to adopt her. Nita was very scared to get in the big Camioneta pickup truck because she was so hyper and when the truck started to move Nita began barking wildly but Ducon hugged her until her fears went away. It was love at first sight

So Amanda's husband Fidel drove Ducon and Nita to the Temuco Airport where Nita was put into her crate for the two hour flight to Santiago. Ducon retrieved her from the baggage area and off to the Cargo area of Santiago de chile airport they walked together with Nita on a leash, she had been walked a few times on a leash in pucon. So there was no problem except that Ducon was not fluent in Spanish and he needed seven additional stamps at the Airport in order to ship her Lan cargo. Suddenly in the dark he met a man with a taxi who had come to find him and assist them both to the dog friendly Santiago Hotel Hindenleben but the plan had changed now somewhat as Nita was once again placed in her crate with water and dog food including sedative pills to help her sleep during the nine hour flight to New York, USA. So Johnny the taxi driver really saved the day and all the stamps to the documents were in order fifteen minutes before takeoff ten hours after arriving from Temuco. Nita was now flying to North America, USA. Ducon Pucon went off with Johnny to Hindenleben for a nights rest as was to fly to Lima the next afternoon.

So Nita landed in New York, much to the displeasure of Ducon Pucon's father who's first thought had been.

Why not adopt a puppy in the town you live in Ducon? But this became irrelevant now. Ducon's godson Ducon Futon was on his way to New York from New Hampshire, Nita's final destination. Ducon Futon had his friend with him Kevin Fisherman and they were going to pick up Mayra Nicaragua his former girlfriend who was fluent in Spanish and could read the instructions stamps credentials and requirements for the pickup of Nita, everything written in Spanish from Chile which no one in homeland security could translate because Puerto Rico has a different dialect. After seven hours of Mayra screaming at customs officials Nita was stamped for official entry into the United States of America tested to see if she was a bomb or full of cocaine and finally in the car with Kevin Fisherman and Ducon Futon and whisked away onto the super highways to New Hampshire despite objections of Mayra who decided she loved the dog more since it understood Spanish not English.

So upon arrival in New Hampshire Nita immediately escaped and ran off into the woods chased deer and porcupines and skunks but became hungry by nightfall and reappeared in the yard of the house of Ducons Futons Pucons to meet the domesticated two larger black male dog's brothers to each other, Tank and Charles. Who thought how nice it is to have a female to hump.

Let it be said that Nita Jovencita Bonita put the boy dogs in their places with consecutive streetfighter nips to their ears and eyeballs. Nita is no normal domestic pet she is from the wilds of Volcano Rukapillan, translated means house of a devil. She is from Patagonia not New England. This went on for several weeks. Luckily within days Ducon pucon flew back from Lima, Peru and was reunited with this wonderful pet friend because all of them are!

Now her ears no longer point upward like a wolf but droop down and she is a happy dog in her new home where she is loved beyond measure. This should be the fate of every homeless dog and every homeless person. Let the world be a better place YOU CAN MAKE A DIFFERENCE!

Go therefore and feed the hungry, shelter those with no roof. Be a better person and make this world a nice place. It was thought once by almost each and every young delinquent that nice old people were weak, that loving people with soft hearts are suckers and idiots.

Let God be your judge if your hearts are hardened He will destroy you but if you find a place and a home for LOVE he will add you to the living and you will have a new home with God and enter into the covenant of the living! You will breathe fresh air and health you will value more than money because now you will receive God's gift, love, and pass it along.

THE SPARK OF LIFE

There was given to me a spark of life by God

A flame of love inside me given by God

Let it be not diminished or I will wilt and die

I might nickname it Jesus because it came from God

It is pure and innocent as a lamb and the source of life itself

When I die it shall return to God from Whom it came

My own subconscious mind pays tribute to it

Every living thing acknowledges these sparks as heaven sent

The great pines and lobsters beneath the sea know of it

If I would be an atheist I would be in denial of it

Why would I deny my own life to live in hate like a wretched communist?

Cigarettes are a jealous imitation of it sent by the devil

It is more a magnetic spark held in a magnetic field

Jesus had great magnetism and everyone he touched was reignited

Reignite me please my God and Savior, reignite Your Holy Spark in me

That may live all my days to fulfill Your Divine Plan and give glory to You

For this Your marvelous Creation we thank You for Everything

That by Your Our Grace You have found us worthy to be Your servants

I LOVE THAT..

I love that the full moon rises over Agiocochook (Mt. Washington) to the east\\

I love that it sets over tiny Mount Eustis

So much that I howl at it in imitation of my hound dogs

I love that God has given me life

It is from God our father from Whom we all sprang forth to live

Some men think Jesus was God or maybe Krishna was Divine?

They do not hurt me so let them be, let them continue to believe I

realize the flame of God's love is now in me

Why should I contest this, why should I let it flicker

In immorality and sin, it might become just dark smoke?

Let my candle burn bright for all men in all of the nations to marvel

Let them remember that all our lives are holy and consecrated

We are sent here from our very God to rise up and stand

I stand tall and proud to salute my flag

My love is rekindled in me to love this land where I live Because

to hate it is to be diminished by negativity and doubt So I pledge

allegiance to my moral God

Who permits me to live each new day in righteousness

Anything less will endanger me and lessen my happiness I

am happy that I love...it is God's gift to us all

It warms my heart because my heart belongs to God

My heart, my mind and my soul - may all three of you live on

Thus when our president says stupid things, lies and or makes wrong

ecisions

I know and trust that he too will be held accountable for any evil

The meek shall inherit...whatever is left

GUERNICA, AN INDICTMENT OF UTOPIA,

Perhaps it was a spiritual illness
Called Marxism-Leninism
Whose original proponents were possessed?
By some industrial demons?

Born in squalid conditions
These poor imagined there might be a Utopia
In some faraway place called heaven-on-earth
Where all men and women would be brothers-sisters
In a workers' paradise with huge smokestacks

Even so death is required to gain access there-martyrdom
One needs to be lined up, shot and buried in a ditch
So the many poor and homeless were lined up accordingly
Perhaps given a last cigarette but more likely their pockets emptied
Their last cigarettes stolen from them
By men with machine guns claiming to have been sent by the Pope
Whosoever fears for his life fears all these wretches
Will there ever be justice for the poor when pigs will fly?

Who is this who claims the right to kill another
Is he not a devil himself as well?
The rich men are favored by God, they are His anointed

Chosen to do God's work to vanquish the poor for their uncleanliness

To punish them for their sins
To cleanse the earth of their iniquities

Because they are all thieves who imagine
That what is mine or yours should belong to them instead. Their fingers are sticky like glue, they are corrupted
They have fallen into an empty hole of atheism
So let the devil save them if he shall choose to
Though the devil saves no one, only Christ will save us

So abandon those who have lost God's blessing
Planes are coming to drop napalm on them
To burn into hell all the disbelievers
Believe instead that God can save your rotten soul
Your one God who loves you, return to him
His arms are ready and waiting to embrace you
When you shall return to your cross ready for Salvation

There may be no mercy for you here on this earth
But Heaven is willing and patiently awaits
Your return to dwell with Angels
Marx was a devil and Hitler his disciple

I know you thought you deserved a better life
A better life than the one you reaped
What you sowed was madness
Because your own parents were tempted
To lie to you for your protection

The truth was hidden from you
That Jesus loves you no other
The only gift from Heaven His Eternal Love

Is all you need to accept not Marx
Not Engels not Mao and Stalin
So return to Golgotha come to the cross
Which is prepared for you also

That where He is in Heaven you may be also
To be with Him Who loves us
We are incapable of love only greed

Turn away from greed and selfish desire
To serve Him Who sent you here
To serve lovingly the One who sent you
Let His love fill your heart with joy
Be most compassionate and kind
So that when you see a beggar give

Give all you have to give with joy
When they shall ask you for help
Then you shall rescue them from despair
They shall all see we are Christians by our love, charity, hope and faith
We who are the merciful are not haughty

We do not run around with our noses stuck up
We condescend and make friends
With those less fortunate with the poor
The homeless, the orphans and the widows
We shall console them in their sorrows and be Godly

We talk of God with gladness
He loves us all and can save us
From this pit into which we were born
We will rise up from the ashes
We will rise up to see Him

Though we were dead we shall
Be resurrected by the thought of Him
Our God Who loves us and so we receive
In order to give freely
This love of His that came to us we pass it along

To those less fortunate than us they fill the streets
They are window shopping on the sidewalks

Yet what is displayed in windows cannot save them
Although chocolate goes a long way
To make us more loving and restore us

It is our God (God's love) Who bakes the cake
Who kneads the dough and adds the water of Life That it may
rise to feed us these fresh loaves of bread
It is not a right to be fed, it is a privilege of the deserving of the Lord
Though they sow their fields the harvest is not guaranteed
Be thankful for what you have
And do not imagine you need your neighbor's wife or car as well

Be content and not led into temptation
Do not think what others have belongs to you
Only God is yours and you are His
Seek salvation first and everything shall be added to you
We are all monks and nuns,fathers and mothers
We are the stewards of this creation given to us

Therefore be responsible
The heathen are not

LISTEN TO THE WORD OF GOD THAT HE IS GOOD

O mortal man, why do you hate?

It profits you nothing to hate your mortal destiny, you shall die regardless

Your loving God allows you to return to the dust from which you came,

From which you grew up to be vibrant and full of joy that you live

Even more so should you rejoice in your immortal body?

Because God might reward you with eternal life through him

If you shall believe in love, his love that he died for your sins upon that cross

In order to prepare for you a place where he has gone you might be also

Though you must believe in love that it comes from God and may enter you

To destroy all hatred and fear forever, they are the same as doubt and death

So rise up from defeat and destruction, rebuild your city from its ashes

Rebuild the walls inside your heart and so love everyone and every small thing

Because the loud shall soon cry and the very silent shall utter the truth

So when he speaks to you, listen to the word of God that He alone is good

O mortal man rejoice in God's perfect plan to remove you from mortality

To give you immortality through Him, He comes for you with His Sacred Heart

How he loves you that you might understand through His Grace

That you shall be most graceful as well and appreciative of every small thing of

every small child and every puppy and each tiny kitten let joy fill your heart

Do not kill, do not steal, and do not lie with another man's wife

Do not divorce, do not envy and do not doubt that God loves us all

So the arrogant man points a gun at his own head, do not envy him

Walk softly and be gentle like a summer breeze from offshore

The new time is coming when you shall behold your God, yes you shall see Him

He might even appear to you in the mirror if you shall love yourself by loving others

They are each one of them struggling for his or her freedom from bondage in Egypt

We were all slaves to sin which trapped us in most unfavorable circumstances

Therefore we were arrested for our own good, we were booked into the jail cell

We had so threatened our own safety that we were led into captivity

O immortal God please deliver us back home where we belong with friends and family

Our children and pets miss us so and long for our return

Let us greet them all with open arms and open hearts and speak the truth

That God saves us always and has never failed to do so

Never failed to do so, never never and will always rescue us forever

Why didn't you believe this your entire life? Why did you doubt the truth?

Because you lied you became lost you would not admit your errors and sins

Confess them now to God, my dear God I do confess that I have been tempted by darkness

I do confess that I am lost because I was led in a wrong direction away from you

Listen to the Word of God that He alone is good and that your salvation

is in proximity to Him so sing praise and dance for joy.

He has never failed to liberate the captives and He can lead you home

where you belong with Him forever

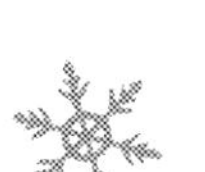

WE ALL KNOW WHAT LOVE IS SO WE ALL KNOW JESUS

We all know Jesus and what love is. He is in our subconscious. He is in our DNA. He is our blueprint for success and prosperity.

Those who are in denial have serious problems, not just with God but with themselves. Why would anyone want to be in conflict with his or her inner self? Such a path would be self-destructive almost suicidal.

Therefore it is imperative to follow God's commands because God is inside us as well as every living thing. We need to live in harmony and peace. So be quiet and listen to your inner voice.

THERE MUST BE REASON

Whereupon the realtor saleslady had a husband who was a locksmith

Therefore the perpetual tourist said to her,

"I have been locked out of my cabin for ten years because I lost the key to my house!" "I will tell my clever husband to go pick the lock for you, if you list the property for sale at an attractive price since you made no improvements to it!"

"I would like to sell it for a million dollars!" replied the owner.

The unlucky clever husband was summoned but could not complete the work because he died.

So the perpetual tourist remained just that and continued making his monthly payments for the house he could not live in.

There must be a moral to this iconic story, let's imagine one.

Why did the stranger want to buy a house he could not live in?

Did he purposely wish to be a homeless fool and idiot or is there some special hidden meaning to this puzzle?

Let's ask God in heaven for an answer!

Dear God in heaven, sorry to wake you up right now, were you sleeping? Excuse us for asking

About the house of Israel which came into possession by some madman

He dared not live there under that roof due to his forgetfulness

Just what did he forget to do and why was he destined to lose the key?

This is like the story of the messiah who was sent into the native land of God's chosen people

He was dressed quite meagerly in a long white gown to match the bride but she could not be found

She remained hidden behind her clouds like a holy city, like a diadem too bright to be seen without going blind

So why did the groom come to find her? Was it time for the very great wedding? Surely he must have proposed to her but now she remained hidden in a veil of clouds like a smokescreen.

Is she on fire, is she burning and why?How can this problem be solved?

"I see the man has lost his family and been cast out into the wilderness to find God

Who dwells there in a remote place under a broom tree that has now caught on fire

Go and preach unto the distant counties like a lost tourist and say unto everyone you meet,

"The messiah is coming soon but the bride is not yet ready and must be prepared accordingly"

"She must adorn herself in a white long flowing gown like the groom"
"He is coming soon though we know not the hour it is near"

"Make his house ready and open its door to a very lost tourist!"

God indeed will be lost upon the planet Earth why won't he stay in heaven?" There must be a reason, perhaps there is a devil in the white house

So is the Lord Almighty coming in person (the Ominous Day of the Lord or is he sending someone to warn us once again of that day?

FLYING FREE

Jul 28, 2018. 10:36 AM

O how we so long to be loved!

Is it not the driving force of life itself?

But to be loved is to love others, or to not love is to choose self' destruction and death.

We try to accomplish many great things, we manipulate to acquire fame, fortune and reputation in the world.

We stand in a great spotlight upon a grand stage and sing as though in an opera,

But a solo song is the blues and we turn blue, we need to be in harmony with a chorus,

The chorus is those who love us and care for us,

Because we are now in sync with the greater human goal,

To love for love's sake!

So visit the prisoners and feed the hungry, give shelter to the homeless,

To those that are begging give them at least pennies nickels and dimes

And when a friend asks us for something, give them double

When one asks for a shirt give them two.

Those who steal shall be stolen from, those who cheat only cheat themselves, only lovers are to be admired and those who cannot are tossed into that great sea of despair where waves crash against their boats driving them shipwrecked unto a rocky island

So love your neighbor as you would want to be loved

Because you are soon going away in a small vessel to another universe where they will weigh your love not your money (because all your money you have acquired reflects only your selfishness and lack of love) it weighs down your boat so that you have lost your freedom and mobility to be happy.

You can only be faithful without money for what it brings is temptation and rebellion, so go to the casino and gamble it away or put it in the bank, you are better off with just a little or none. So spend it on clothes and food so you will not be naked cold or starving. But share with those less fortunate. Work because you love what you do not because you love money

Have pity and compassion on all animals and feed the hungry, and have compassion for all plants because they need water and sunlight much as you do also,

And be happy.....

And sing all of this as you walk and you will be followed

Because now you are following Jesus

You are marching triumphantly

Into the sanctuary of Jerusalem, the walled city

To be with God

PART 2

LEGENDARY INFERNO SKI RACER AND WINNER

Sun, Jun 16, 7:18 AM

1969

Inferno part two

A week before(the Legendary race down Tuckerman's Ravine, New Hampshire)/The Mafia kidnapped him/But having to brain/He decided to sign up with them/They gave him a suitcase full of drugs to sell/He took them all himself instead/Superman and Clark Kent he climbed a High Building set to fly/Did he ever come down? No, I don't think so/Some skiers are legends/Yes some legends in their own minds/And some skiers are legends out of their minds/He bought a motorcycle/And liked riding it in the fog/On an invisable Road/Seemingly going Nowhere/Above the Clouds/Finally he crashed his 63 Thunderbird on Vail Pass in a blizzard/ Now He pushes up the Daisies/In his hometown he is forgotten

DIRTY WAR

Dirty War! War is much worse than dirty

A full bath with shampoo and suds cannot take away such filth

It is more like a chronic illness of the mind

Such an agony is felt lifelong like an unclean conscience

The killing never stops and finally the killer turns upon his own sick self...

What can I easily explain to those of you who are not history majors?

You would need to have been there to feel what I have felt and seen what I saw in Argentina as Peron was losing his grip on power, died but his legacy lived on to haunt us with his viciousness like some ravenous wolf that enters the flock not to eat but just to kill and keep killing.

The Spanish Civil War of 1937 was just part of a war that began when Hannibal crossed from Africa to fulfill a promise made to his dying father on his deathbed to attack Rome Southern Europe was attacked from Africa and overrun with elephants and cattle with bundles of flaming sticks tied to their horns: Fatschis. It wasn't very long before they proclaimed their own version of the One God called Islam.

Europe converted to Christianity even so, this was not just a religious war, and this was a war of races. When Hitler came to power, it was nothing new and original. This war had lasted for centuries and millenniums under different banners perhaps. Nevertheless, it was the same dirty war which continued after resting phases called peace or peace in our time etcetera. It was the same war for centuries almost unstoppable. It employed millions of men in vast armies with vast armaments in production to capture vast train loads of booty to feed the starving children and mothers. It was a war for the economy as well and kept populations in check until the invention of the United Nations which became an overseer but had no solution to this planet's stifling over population.

Because I was no longer a child, I was approached by knowledgeable adult soldiers. Some wore uniforms but even more did not. They were all fighters and they all knew or sensed the reality of racial war. Most had seen death either in their own families or firsthand on the front.

In Argentina every year they gather all the mothers of those thousands of their own children who disappeared "Los Desaparecidos". They were arrested by police and given flu shots which drugged them unconscious. Then were loaded like cord wood onto helicopters and dropped into the Atlantic Ocean several miles out. A few of their bodies washed upon the beaches unrecognizable of course, but most sank with weights attached.

In Latin America there are many native Indians who mostly are not wealthy and being such they become the adherents of left wing politics including Marxism and Communism even though it is godless humanism, it preaches that men must break from Catholic restraints that advocate and bless poverty and suffering in order to join a grand industrialization for the benefit of all brothers in a shared Utopia. The leaders of these cults of men include ruthless mob bosses and gangsters of the worst kind and in the case of Salvador the savior Allende he was an incredible wife beater I am told.

Added to these perpetual losers are a handful of Mohammedans or Musselmanes ie. Muslims who during the Inquisition of Ferdinand were ordered to leave Spain even though their families had been there three hundred years. They were to choose between Holland or the New World which offered gold and more adventure so they came across the ocean and arrived, although bitter perhaps.

Then from the Spanish Civil War of 1937 came the losers, the communists all sponsored with boat passages by Stalin himself who wanted them to create new cells of comrades in the Americas.

When they put the last final cigarette in my mouth after burning my wrist and fingernails and then pointed the pistol in my nostrils, it became obvious to me that since I was now sixteen years of age, I would have to choose a side to be on, either the rich or the poor? Where would I stand and fight The rich had all the guns and bullets and the poor were lined up against a wall.

A machine gun was placed in my hands and I was ordered to shoot. I had to pull the trigger or I would be shot. They yelled at me to shoot. The men at the wall yelled at me to shoot at the men who were ordering me. I pulled the trigger again but nothing happened.

"The gun is jammed!" I protested. They laughed because I had not been given a loaded gun in case I switched sides suddenly. They just wanted to know where my heart was.

I was pulled aside and Fritz stepped up his gun loudly burping and the cries of the dying

ACADIAN

A man lives not by bread alone but by every word that comes from God. Indeed all words have been born from our Creator. Apparently just as the eastern coast of North America is sinking into the Atlantic Ocean, a new Tectonic plate to the east is rising above it to create Acadia, a steep, mountainous island.

The old world passes away and a new one is rising over it. It is time to forget the follies of youth and all the energy wasted on passion, an illusory great disappointment to concentrate on the new man or woman promised to us by our savior and lord, J.C., thus let us abandon the agony and despair of false doctrines and concentrate instead on what is hopeful and true, modest and contrite because our individual time remaining on this earth is running out like grains of sand in the hour glass.

So let us concentrate our remaining energy on the life sustaining emotion of love which we have received most graciously from God through our mothers and fathers in order to share such a God given blessing to make this earth a brighter happier place

Dear Ian,

I am writing you on behalf of your mother Susan Ellen Bradshaw concerning her lawsuit against the State of Rhode Island.

It is quite apparent to me that she is an angel sent from God into this world. Please treat her with respect even though she is not of this world.

Someday possibly, you will be an angel also and finally be reunited with her in Heaven. She is doing a very good job up here hanging stars and directing planets and everyday people in their struggles on earth a very demeaning existence there with governments which steal people's children away from them for a variety of reasons both legal and illegal.

There is some misunderstanding of the laws down there which were passed to protect all the people but which protect more the incomes of lawyers and judges who have been corrupted.

Through no fault of her own your mother lost custody of you because she was severely beaten up physically and went to the Emergency Room and then the psychiatric Hospital as well. Her condition remains unstable but has nothing to do with how much she loves you.

She loves you immensely and forever, so does God in Heaven also! Your mother had no choice but to enter a convent of nuns where she scrapes and mops floors all day long while she thinks constantly about you. She misses you immensely and completely. Such is the life of any angel but your mother is a special angel you call,

Mommy, I miss you!

Yes you do, Ian. Everyone misses his or her mommy. Soldiers wounded on the battlefields of every major war cry out when they are wounded mortally,

Mommy, Mommy!

This is an evil world planet earth and it is run by the devil himself. I am so sorry that the Rhode Island court judge is an evil witch first class reincarnated from the Salem witch trials where she was burned at the stake for feminism rightfully. This is a man's world Ian, and you will be a big man someday soon and maybe even a lawyer or a judge and be powerful with lots of money which will be made by inflicting pain and suffering on the masses.

I am happy you are somewhat content with your new family found for you by the State of Rhode Island founded by Roger Williams, a religious clairvoyant. Unfortunately religious conscience has been lost by this modern governmental machine of oppression to squeeze out the blood of the people in the winepress of sacrilegious wrath that flows like a river into Narragansett Bay which is now red from this Red Tide.

All my apologies to you, son, from your bereaved mother who it is obvious is no longer of this earth as she has no material roots for her defense which is strictly angelic.

Eventually, God will hear your prayers in Heaven so please pray to Jesus Christ as He is your Redeemer and the plan is for your salvation from the many evils of the world which are increasing daily. As there is such extreme overpopulation now it seems necessary to confine all people in a system of slavery called humanism.

Everyone on Earth is suffering and there is no exception to the mortal human condition except for a few seconds of joy found in music or sports or fine dining and humor. However most of the humor on Earth is sadistic including the sadistic ritual of judges in many courtrooms.

Unfortunately, Ian, you have been diagnosed with angelic behavior resembling too often the joviality of your biological mother, Susan Ellen Bradshaw who has been found guilty of laughing...and more specifically of laughing at the stern comical sadistic judge which is called contempt of court.

Up here in Heaven we mostly ski and play tennis or go to the beach. We do this somehow without large sums of money amazingly. Our dogs and cats accompany us everywhere. But you, Ian, cannot come here just yet as you have an earthly life to live and your birth father has been petitioning the court for parental rights and guardianship,

We don't have the ultimate authority there on Earth as it is run by a lot of demons, bigots and hypocrites so you will have to be patient while God tries to work this out in order for true Justice to prevail.

Your mother has been moved to an asylum where she does the Rosaries constantly mumbling prayers for the salvation of all of us. She is a very religious woman with drugs and alcohol and partying with bad associates of the past all left behind on that trash dump called the Earth.

Just remember to pray constantly and think of her because she is in the Bible too.... "And I saw a woman with a child in the wilderness....."

TAMSIN

Mon, Sep 28, 2015

I brought one of my dates to softball night at Cliff Crosby Stadium under the lights in Franconia and struck out seven times consecutively, a new town record. Her name she claimed was Tamsin and she claimed that I slept with her thirty years ago at an overnight wild hippy party in Intervale while somebody's parents were absent. I can't seem to quite remember unless maybe her name back then was Tammy and I do remember the house and that Brad Boynton had organized it.

Tammy's main problem in her young life had been her more slender shapely sister whose white Finnish skin with blonde hair applied eyelashes and hot red lipstick exceptionally well so any boy coming over to the house desired the hot younger sister who was actually cold as a fish and despised almost everybody as inferior.

Our love became rekindled when I saw her in the Jackson Inn bar where she was now a cocktail waitress. Tammy was in no way petite and large boned body and prominent forehead did not look good in red lipstick so she used pink lipstick

Tammy claims mostly to be of French Canadian descent, her father having been the very mild mannered congenial postmaster of Jackson named Ward Freeman and of course she had a brother Ward junior Freeman. The mother having migrated off the boat from Finland evidently didn't ever tell the children where she had come from as Finland had allied itself with Germany during the Finno-Russian War 1939 when the Russians decided to capture it they were driven back.

So thirty years after our original sin, Tamsin would now drive over Crawford Notch to see me have dinner and then immediately sex, sex and more sex. She is to this day the last woman I ever slept with as shortly thereafter I had between twenty seven and one hundred Dalmations.

The dogs would not accept any future girlfriends as they insisted on sleeping in the bed with me, on top of the bed with me, on top of me etc.

I had a very small cabin in Twin Mountain and the six dogs back then went wild with every visit barking jumping up at her nibbling at her heels like she was indeed some delicious pork chop thrown into their midst. I had neighbors with whom I didn't get along terribly well as they ran a Day Care Center for small children mostly afraid of dogs. The woman over there was a blond with big teats and of course the Town Cop was over there trying to work his way into her life.

Tamsin was very gargantuan and would crawl on top of me and smother me with all her love the dogs trying to avoid all our contortions as the bed itself taking up most of the space the small cabin had to offer. Of course she was the best of all the women I had ever been consumed by.

One night at the locally bar which has since been torn down because there was a fight every five minutes and one time they had actually carried me to the door on all their shoulders and tossed me when I had not so much as even thrown a punch, Tamsin decided to mickey me with maybe ecstasy for her pleasure. But of course next morning when I woke up I realized my prized new possession a handwritten hand bound book containing pictures of Napoleon Bonaparte at age 7,11,15,18,23,26,29,33 with commentary all in French...it was missing and Tamsin had disappeared with it leaving a note to the effect that I had too much baggage.

Of course I had suitcases all over the lawn and in the woods and under tarps and in small additions I had built on the cabin that were now even larger, three stories high in fact! But the very prized special hand bound book I had discovered in the basement used bargains at Three of Cups, Joanne kenneys store and paid three dollars for just two months hence was probably worth thousands of dollars and behold I heard through the grapevine Tamsin had then taken her mother on vacation to Istanbul which she adored.

How would I support her anyway from my meager bicycle mechanic wages? So I returned to the softball field where Cliff Crosby was happy to see me and turned on the lights and we played till four in the morning and I only struck out four times with two singles, two doubles, and a triple. But no more home runs as Tamsin was gone leaving me a ruined man.

My house was condemned in Twin Mountain and the Town Cop actually smiled as he said,

"Oh sorry to inform you; the town has decided not to accept your check for the building permit: they have in fact turned down your application. Michael Ward my attorney in Littleton asked what in the world had possessed me and not realizing exactly the abundant quantities of acid that Tamsin had put in my every drink I replied,

"Jesus came into my life and He Himself built all those additions on my house!" The sellers were gearing up to suit me for the expected bill the town would soon hand them for the cleanup and demolition. I was five months late on payments to them anyway; Why not have some fun in life anyway? So I went to the Courthouse in Lancaster and quitclaimed my interest in the property to my fiancé in Colorado, Dawn Feehan and I was off the hook loaded my now twenty seven Dalmations in the car and drove out west. Well I gave away a few of the newborn puppies before leaving so the number was slightly less

FRANCONIA DOG STORY 20A

Sun, Nov 24, 2013, 2:29PM

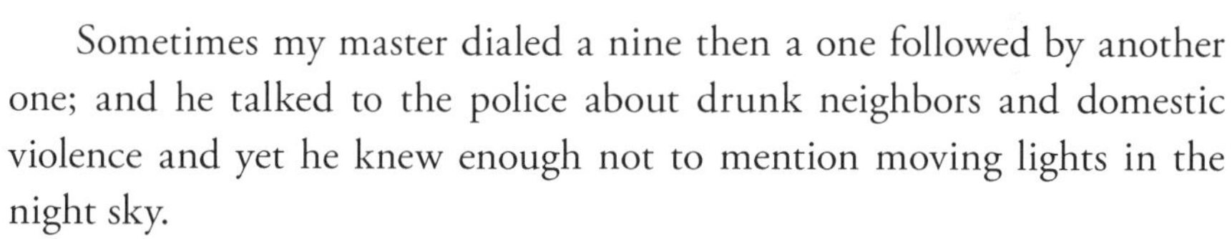

Sometimes my master dialed a nine then a one followed by another one; and he talked to the police about drunk neighbors and domestic violence and yet he knew enough not to mention moving lights in the night sky.

Most of the time he did not prefer talking to police in general as this would mean trouble followed by even more TROUBLE!

So he picked up the public pay phone in Twin Mountain one September morning and thought out loud,

"It is best to call Erika Koo as she always knows what's going on today!" So he did. Ring. Ring."

"This is Erika, yes, oh finne us yes; come right over as the Trade Center Tower in New York City is on fire!"

My master replied,

"Oh they tried to bomb it again, from the subway?" He hung up the phone and drove to Mrs. Koo's small cabin in the Sprucewood.

"See it there on the television!" She exclaimed opening the door and pointing at the television.

"Oh my god it's really burning" We dogs could hear him say from inside the cabin. There were some loud exclamations to follow!!!

"Oh my God, a plane has just crashed into the second tower! "All of this in New York City not far from Wall Street where Egbert might be.

We dogs had been driven through that city once in a rush hour traffic jam so we pulled off the Haarlem exit to watch teenagers playing basketball with on looking parents at outdoor Haarlem park Courts. Then at the first stoplight leaving a young man in another car revving its engine pulled a gun to muffle the sound of shots about to be fired. Why Finneus didn't even wait for that red light to change, hitting the accelerator we left that New York City, my only impression of the place; people there get quite excited all the time and now a lot more excitement with airplanes crashing into tall buildings: perhaps the World Is Coming To An Enda big cloud of smoke now forming over New York City a kind of Shroud or veil to protect it perhaps.

Suddenly Tower One collapsed.

"Oh no! The other tower will collapse too!" said my master. It did just a few minutes later as predicted.

Then a plane crashed into the Pentagon in Washington, D.C. Then a plane crashed in Pennsylvania.

My master loaded us dogs in the pickup and with Mrs. Koo still devoted to her T.V. we left for Vermont to see if it was still there; and we stopped rest assured at Cochran Family Ski Mountain.

All we dogs ran to the summit where we found young Jimmy Cochran working there. He just kept working wondering why we were so excited and where we had come from.

My master stayed below talking to Mrs. Virginia the mother Cochran who was smoking a marijuana cigarette called a "Reefer" and offered my master some which he declined.

"Thank you anyway!" he had told her. Poor Mrs. Virginia she had medical prescribed marijuana to ease her pain from that awful cancer. meanwhile Roofer did not return to the mountain base as he became strongly attached to Jimmy Cochran who was feeding him some leftovers from his lunchpail. so we all spent that night sleeping in the truck in the empty parking lot of that world class ski resort, waiting for Roofer with his very short Corgi type legs to finally walk all the way down that long mountain.

The next place we stopped on the highway people were watching a television with a picture live of the President of the United States of America: and he said,

"We're going to find you, we're going to hunt you down and bring to justice the perpetrators of these awful attacks against unarmed civilians."

"So run and hide you awful terrorists because your days are numbered" said my master.

TUCKERMAN'S RAVINE

My father and godfather Bill Keazy who also attended Yale University took me on my first adventure to Tuckerman's Ravine. I was eight years old in 1956.There were a lot of rocks on the hiking trail. Puddles of water and waterfalls but I was tiring quickly on the 2.4 mile climb to Hojos which they explained to me was a Howard Johnson's restaurant where I would be rewarded by ice cream.

I went again at age ten with my father up the Glen Boulder trail. I was having difficulty again and my father suspected there was indeed something wrong with my health. It was my irregular thyroid gland: I suffered hyperthyroidism as a child.

At fourteen I went with my Holderness classmates on a ski trip up there to discover the Ravine was closed due to falling idea poor leader, I led my closest friends up there to almost get hit by giant ice balls the size of cars. We left hurriedly as we had come. It had been very foggy and the ice balls were only visible when we followed mysterious tracks in the snow to find one.

So by age fifteen I considered myself a veteran on that peak Mt. Washington even though I had been to its summit only three times. My father was busy doing business in the city and my governess Caroline and her family had gone to England to meet the Queen because of all their involvement in the Salvation Army.

Thus my father employed an Austrian ski instructor,Heinz, studying economics who was employed by Sugarbush Ski Area,Vermont to be my babysitter for a month. We went up to the Ravine and skied four runs and Heinz announced he was now ready for Martha's Vineyard as he was a horndog and had a girlfriend there with rich parents. I expressed disinterest and wanted to spend another week skiing up there although it was already May and compared to Austria the skiing was very limited and disinteresting to him.

"Well, I am leaving!" he announced. Excellent I thought. We made a deal that he would return and pick me up in a few weeks but not to tell my father anything. I agreed. He never returned. So essentially now I was a runaway child on that big mountainside. I stored my sleeping bag and rucksack in a lean-to. Sully was the forest ranger in charge there. I informed him that I would be staying four more days whereupon Heinz would return for me. He was hesitant but after a few beers with buddies he acquiesced. Off I went on a big mountain ski adventure to return to my lean-to quite tired. My sleeping bag was gone and a bunch of college students were drinking beer.

One of them claimed to be from Dartmouth but perhaps this was a bad joke. He said his bag was big enough for both of us. I was cold and tired my thyroid having crapped out: I was shivering and going into shock as it was snowing by now. He said I could use his bag that I could crawl in so I did and the lights went out. I woke up the next day and was looking for my clothes. Everyone had left. I found them and put them on. But I was hurt. I didn't go skiing but did find my backpack and sleeping bag. Then I found Sully who said.

"Welcome to the White Mountains!" and offered me a sip of beer. I took two. He grabbed the bottle back. I found people leaving who gave me their food rather than carry it down the mountain. I stayed there until July fourth and the patch of snow was by now very small and a passerby hiker noticed me and said,

"Where's your father?" He then took me to Sully and demanded to call the State Police. My father drove up from New York about eight hours and said, "Where is Heinz?"

TAKE YOUR GIRLFRIEND TO EUROPE

Sat, Oct 21, 2017, 1:11AM

This is another sad tale about young love or summer love that blows in with the breeze and then the wind shifts and guess what?

Well I did it, I took my girlfriend to Europe and we bicycled across the Rhine as the sun set in mid-September and there was a grand ball at some riverside hotel and we switched partners and I was dancing with a young frauline who thought I felt strange, finally after the dance she realized I was a foreigner but not before and the music kept playing a slow waltz and I pulled her closer beneath a blue moon in broken clouds, schoene freude!

So in a different episode I did recall to her being in a teepee in Steamboat Springs with an Indian squaw who brought me home from the bar of the hotel where we the U.S. Ski Team were staying with Billy kidd and Bob Beattie.

"This is all our sacred land they are developing into a ski area. It has been stolen from us!" she was very bitter and her father and uncle had died probably from whiskey or moonshine after having served in the Second World War in combat to defend America...

My fraulein didn't quite understand my story about all us American Indians. Meanwhile my girlfriend made some contacts with several Barons who owned distant castles and Mercedes so she decided to retire the bicycle and me for the duration. I kept pedaling in the pouring rain to the point where I became homeless wet with pneumonia and a high fever so my mind was not working properly but luckily a Mormon sister took notice of my poverty and deranged homelessness leading me to an empty bed in some monastery. My girlfriend was having the time of her life sleeping from bed to bed but gaining no long lasting respect. Finally I did meet her and she confessed she would stay in Europe a little longer, just another month, and miss the plane ride home with me which I had purchased for us both.

But these were not cozy times at least for me. She had a silken pussy and I did not. Doors opened for her but banged shut in my face. We did get back together for an impoverished destitute North American winter staring out our one lonely window at a hayfield in Missouri Heights above Carbondale, Colorado where our car had broken down and it was a four mile walk to town but nothing was there save a bar and a grocery store with empty shelves and several cowboys who had fallen off the wagon and their horses too.

When spring came she remembered better times overseas and that over there no snowy winters were to be had except in the far distant alps. So she ran away with her lesbian girlfriend away to Ireland never to return except once and I was to meet her and take her back at our rendezvous at JFK International. But I lost her letter with the flight number. And then the car to go to the airport some two hundred sixty miles needed gas and suddenly i ran out of money.

This is life on earth, a forlorn planet of soft crime and worse. The petty criminals are punished with unending suffering from which they learn grace which they will need to enter heaven, a better place than here I am told where the streets are paved with gold.

Amen

"YOUNG PRO SKI RACER" HARD FAST LIFE IN THE ROCKIES"

2019

I was a young pro ski racer with International Ski Racers Association when I traveled to Aspen, Colorado in 1972. I was ranked tenth overall and sixth in slalom with winnings of $6,500 which was more than enough to buy a cheeseburger and beer special at Pinocchio's Restaurant where the waitresses wore short skirts and low cut blouses for big tips and mine had big ones and a friendly smile, probably from drinking from a flask on the job but that didn't matter to me at all.

She had auburn reddish hair and told me her mother was Swedish from Stockholm (actually more Danish).This was close enough for me and going home to her trailer because I was homeless: this was heaven and she was the goddess herself though possible a drinker, was I to complain?

Young pro ski racers or young amateur ski racer was really a title given to all of us who loved the sport of skiing back then. There was no freestyle and no snowboarding, and no super giant slalom just three alpine events and three gold medals every four years in the Olympics which was televised. It was the sport of rich white children who went on family vacations including Christmas to snow covered hills where the children mostly skied and the adults mostly got drunk and told wild stories.

Actually it was the year before in 1971 when I first met Phyllis Garrett whose parents had moved from Indiana to Grand Junction. My homeless winter wandering separated us seasonally because I still lived in New Hampshire but wanted to live in the west like my rich friend John Stirling whose parents had just died leaving him four million dollars, including land in Florida, apartments in California, over a hundred acres on Missouri Heights in Carbondale, Colorado and a very small cabin with no plumbing in Aspen where the ski industry was now thriving and tearing up the old wooden sidewalks of its past mining era and replacing them with concrete, even paving the once mud streets. That was real western clay mud, at least five pounds stuck under each boot sole.

I managed to tip my waitress a hundred dollar bill which is like a few thousand dollars now. She was a saloon gal and we moved together to Telluride in 1974 where I finally landed a job, racing director, and she was a cocktail waitress at the former brothel at the east end of town where they even gave her free drinks and kept her there till 1 am or later. I was not terribly happy about it and disappeared into the Sheraton Hotel for five days with Franny. Phyllis was not happy about that maneuver either. Of course I managed to ski every day at my job as I was the Nastar Pacesetter. Ski Racing was the big show back then and freestylers were all pot smoking hippy liberals who ate granola and grew beards living in Volkswagen buses.

I soon had nowhere to live without Phyllis's generous rent support and I brought home Chandler to my comfy metal house with no heat, someone had given me a key to it as the owner was away. We froze together one long night with a few in between not sweaty flashes.

After building a pro jump for my racecourse with the ski area chainsaw on the Nastar race hill, the ski area was fined $1,000 dollars by the U.S. Forest Service. I was not going to be rehired, at least they let me know in April. My pay had been very meager indeed as I was considered crazy enough and a fool skier to accept carpenter wages, my own terms. I had left home young with no college but managed to gain a berth on the U.S. Ski Team by winning the Junior Nationals GS though only runner-up in the Downhill.

Bob Beattie, the U.S. Ski Coach now became my parental overseer, a job he was decidedly not too thrilled with after interviewing me he realized I didn't have any maturity whatsoever, that I was mostly a young hound after naked young ladies I did occasionally catch ones my own age, this is an event that lasts only a very few years before reality sets in and finances overcome hormones.

Phyllis's mother chain smoked cigars and pipes, anything she could get her hands on especially after work at her home where she interviewed me a ditch digger and was not very terribly impressed.

So Phyllis started working for the Post Office, a very respectable job her parents bent over backward in her behalf but she still loved alcohol and was late to work more than once. So after I found her and took her binge drinking with my friends from Silverton who had wandered in there from various parts of the world as refugees to local bars that had instructed them about a young pro ski racer that lived at 12,600 feet above Gladstone who might provide quarters for them.

To shorten the story we loaded Phyllis into my car from the sidewalk where she passed out cold and away we drove into the night back up to 12,600 feet elevation where it sometimes doesn't snow in August but sleets hail instead.

Phyllis's mother was ballistic but her father was understanding. She decided to ditch me one evening for Nick Nohava, an ex-convict until she found out about him. She moved into Silverton proper and took a job with some Navaho whose store sold turquoise.

I was very sad to lose Phyllis but really the bottle was destroying her. She went home to never be forgiven by her smoking mother while her two sisters moved out successfully, Ingrid and Christine. Then she went to Alcoholics Anonymous and met some heroin addicts who had gone cold turkey because of New Life Assembly of God. Jesus proceeded to save them all while they recruited lost rich hippy children defrocking them of their trust funds and family inheritances for good cause which became an EXODUS TO TEXAS.

I am no longer a young ski racer. I sold my mining claim in Silverton due to thyroid failure quite possibly triggered by drinking spring water for dishes only that my fellow mom-comrades brought from the nearby Lead Carbonate Mine, abandoned.

I sent some letters to Texas after visiting Phyllis once in Paonia with my ski friend Racer Rob Mulrenan who was impressed with her,

"Well, Doctor," he called me and said, "You have good taste. She has les Grand Tetons" he smiled in a whisper. We were all becoming middle age ski bums which is not such a glorious profession when the snow melts in May.

I never heard one thing from Phyllis except she did RETURN TO SENDER my Christmas in July parcel I sent her from Lake City, Colorado.

There was a note attached, something to the effect, "I am all done with you!"\

Twelve years after Phyllis died, I saw an obituary for us all on

"She was a well-respected member of the community and her church in West, Texas. She has gone to the angels now to be one of them."

We are looking forward to hanging stars with her in heaven, Saint Phyllis. Her God given gift was animal husbandry. She preached the Good News of Salvation to farm animals which immediately fell in love and copulated creating abundance.

She fell in love and married a Dutchman with blond hair who sailed off somewhere. She leaves behind a son, Peter, two sisters and a dog and three cats and several thousand farm animals deeply in love.

All you Bedouins out there wandering over the hills (like skiers) looking for your stray animals, come home to your Father (Family vacation skiing) and hear the Word of God, that He is Good

For in the beginning there was God…

SEL HANNAH'S FARM AND THE TEMPORARY RESURRECTION OF PAUL PFOSI, JR.

Sun, Nov 22, 2015 2:50PM

One of the first jobs I ever got where they took out taxes and all that was at Ski Hearth Farm owned and operated by Sel Hannah. Mark Kiernan was sent out there with me to pick corn but I was too clumsy and broke some stalks so Sel promoted me to bag handler.

The big galoots were usually the bag holders and I qualified though only five foot ten inches.

Sel had a daughter named Joanie and another named Lucy. Joan was a successful ski racer winning a bronze medal in the 1962 FIS so she was a bit aloof. A guy named Larry Collins whose parents owned the farm of the same name in Bath was in love with her head over heels. However Joanie was not the marrying kind evidently and he took off from the airport in Twin Mountain with almost no fuel and then dive bombed straight down onto the runway. He must have been very disappointed indeed as this was listed as a suicide.

He should have loved the nicer sweeter Lucy but she was soon claimed by a Swiss ski coach Hans Pfosi from the Italian side of Switzerland perhaps as his hands were big and rough and politics being what they were; he was soon named Ski School Director at Waterville Valley, New Hampshire which had just been built by the Kennedy's even though officially it was some corporation.

Its president was Tommy Thomas Corcoran whose father had been in the FDR administration as an adviser I seem to recall. Politics as usually they had Frank and Paul Jr and a girl too Eva Pfosi in the middle. But Lucy was mad about something and walked home from the bar after midnight when a car struck and killed her as the fog was so thick. It was a terrible tragedy for the farm which was plagued it seems as Sel's wife the girl's mother Polly had been a terrific skier but came down with polio and never skied thereafter as she was in a wheelchair when I met her. Nevertheless she didn't like me and so I didn't have to go visit her much.

Lucy was so nice that when I backed the truck out the potato cellar with the door open catching the wall and breaking the door off Lucy explained to me it had already been traded in and not to worry.

I was so nervous and felt so bad I had quit that fall around Thanksgiving even though Sel had promised he would take me logging. I surely could have used a new skill as I had none whatsoever.

Sel's mistress another woman in charge of the vegetable garden had me go there in order to remove the weeds but I had hoped a whole row of parsnips so I was relieved of future weeding and mostly had stuck to potato picking which was back breaking work but I was young with a strong back and a dull mind evidently.

Finally a few years later when I had been rehired Paul Jr threw a hay bail on top of my head almost breaking my neck. He was a bit wild and fell in love with Kayla Miller who wouldn't give him the time of day. So he left the bar and drove into a telephone pole one foggy night and they airlifted him to Dartmouth Hitchcock Hospital in Hanover where he was in a coma.

Joanie told me to go there and try to bring him out of the coma so I drove down there arriving about three o'clock in the morning all the Hospital lights out it looked like witches or nurses having a wake with candles up on the third floor.

I yelled out,

"Paul. Paul the Beagle is down to Kelly's (store) and you gotta wake up now and go get it!" as this is what Sel was always yelling at Paul every third morning his whole life.

Lo and behold, Paul's eyes opened up there in Dartmouth Hitchcock Hospital and he said,

"That damn dog is always running down to Kelly's"

So he recovered though with his brain injury he had some minor adjustments one being that he married a Massachusetts woman whose family had a big farm down there in the Connecticut River valley.

So he moved away. His father Paul senior overcome with grief over Lucy's death had flown his single engine plane with no gas in its tank into Lake Tahoe. Nobody had done real well with Sel's daughters but they were actually both sweet nice girls.

Sel had told them they were Norwegians but none in their ancestral tree anywhere but we do know there were a lot of Viking raiders in England. Sel who grew up in Berlin,New Hampshire evidently idolized the Scandinavian ski jumpers who had moved there and built the big ski jump in Milan the very biggest in New Hampshire back in those days it was maybe a sixty meter hill but someone had jumped seventy meters.

It had been a different world back then and Sel claimed in late August of 1934 it had snowed two feet on Mount Washington. Never a dull moment when Sel was near as there would be some story I had never heard before. So skiers had flocked to the farm still to hear his stories and meet Polly Hannah (the ski run Polly's is named after her).

Sel was a partner in Snow Engineering across the street which designed and built Sunday River and Bretton Woods and Sugarloaf and Glen Ellen and Loon, at least according to Sel but there may be some truth to the story somewhere...

PEG

Think I will miss the ski swap. There will be thousands more of them but only one Peg Kenney Siser.

Peg said,

"Come on over and cut the grass at Tamarack" which is the tennis camp in Easton, New Hampshire owned by her and Jack, her husband once New England tennis champion from Dartmouth College.

Then Peg didn't want to pay me the two dollars per hour continually, hoping I might do it for room and board but I replied,

"I need the money, I'm going to South America to ski"

The problem was I had a crush on her sixteen year old daughter, Jo Anne. But Jo Anne had a crush on Graham Hill, son of the U.S. Ambassador to Spain, Robert Hill.

Jo Anne went to St. Mary's Academy in Sugar Hill. I was graduating from Littleton High School in the valley far below. I had made out with her at a party at Ann Gage's house near the Bethlehem exit. We were on top of a bed together but I was too naive perhaps, and Jo Anne, she was just too young still to fall in love. She was at that age still when the girls are fickle.

"He loves me, he loves me not" She was still plucking flowers for the truth.

"If I tell you a secret, will you keep it forever?" she asked me.

"I agreed" but being a boy still I was sure to blabber it on the school bus within a day or two to my best friend Freddy Libby or Ike Sutcliff.

I lived with Goldie Chase on Church Street in Franconia but she had to boot me out at the end of the school year, June 1966.

So Peg knew I had nowhere to go at all and that is why she was offering me a deal because I was now staying with the Monahans on South Street who had five other children. The parents, Leo and Mary worked for the

State Park of New Hampshire at Cannon Mountain. She was in the Cafeteria and he was a lift attendant in winter who drove the bus at the Flume in summer.

Peg said,

"Come out west with us on a ski trip to Arapahoe Basin in Colorado. I had never been there. They loaded all the children in the car to trade in in Detroit for a new station wagon then drove straight to Denver...

"I have to piss," I protested.

"Pee in a cup!" they replied passing me one and telling me to then empty it out the window.

So it was a seven day trip to Arapahoe Basin and Peg and Jack told all us kids to stay on the lift and keep skiing but I got cold and went inside for a hot chocolate and candy bar to shiver still.

"I didn't drive all this way to have you sit indoors! "Peg scolded me and chased me out of the building.

"The sun will come out and warm you, stay on that lift until four o'clock and get your money's worth!"

Gordi Eaton showed up to say hello. He had been promoted to U.S Men's Alpine Coach. He pointed at Breckenridge and told us that that would soon be a ski area too.

Of course Jo Anne stayed home once she learned I had been invited on the trip. Also Billy Kenney did not come with us as he was in Holderness Prep School, with his nose to the books.

Peg was descended from Black Watch of Scotland and Hessian Mercenaries who fought alongside the British redcoats but many defected joining the Rebels.

Peg Kenney Siser, she was Bode Miller's grandmother but this was twelve years before he was even born. The other children were Bubba (Peter),Davy and Ichabod (Mike) a future U.S.Ski Mens ski coach like Gordi Eaton., all of them were younger than me and I was supposed to set an example sneaking into the lodge to eat a candy bar. Oh well.

Peg was born in flat Leavenworth, Kansas in a military hospital but loved snow and wanted to be a ski racer on the Olympic Team. So she moved to New Hampshire where she met Jack at Dartmouth. He had been a runner in the Navy on a battleship in the Battle of Midway in the Pacific.

It was love at first sight.

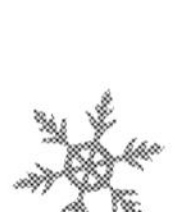

THE LONG ROAD HOME

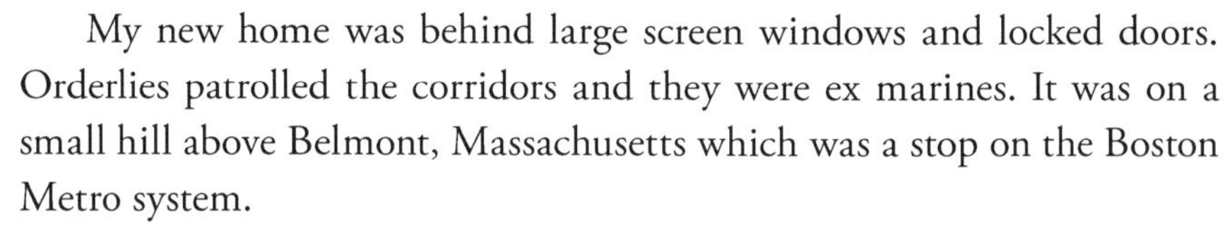

My new home was behind large screen windows and locked doors. Orderlies patrolled the corridors and they were ex marines. It was on a small hill above Belmont, Massachusetts which was a stop on the Boston Metro system.

I placed the token in the slot, opening the bar for me to pass to the lower platform and enter the train to freedom. I was being permitted to pursue my dream of ski racer. I would next board a bus in South Station headed for Plymouth, New Hampshire and Tenney Mountain Ski Area. It was owned by my new host family who would have temporary guardianship of me on these long weekends, John and Hope French. The bus stopped in every small town taking six hours to arrive there. In 1965 there was still no interstate highway to New Hampshire, just old Route 3A and 3B. These weren't bad roads by any standard but the swerved around every tall pine tree and every small pond.

What led to my temporary supervised freedom was Allen Sloan, my shrink. He was actually a very nice guy. I did most of the talking. He inspired me to remember the comfortable past.

There was a lot of stuff my mind already had blocked out. I had been thrown out of my childhood home by my father and stepmother because of my unruliness and tantrums.

I had forgotten, of course, being dressed up by the Chilean Ski Team Chaperone, Mrs. Leatherby, in a long dress with a scarf over my head with lipstick and rouge and bangs. She had to smuggle me by the Nazi Youth in brown shirts from Escuela Militar de La Montana there in Llao-Llao looking for a young American spy.

"She is a deaf indigenous child," Mrs. Leatherby reassured them leading me to the motorboat which would carry us to the Chilean border.

I had to forget hiking to the statue of Christo in Los Andes, Chile with Arab children whose Syrian father warned me that very bad people were asking about my whereabouts, that I was being pursued by Nazis.

I had to forget that I was living in a dirty room on the thirteenth floor of a New York apartment owned by my less than friendly stepmother. I was enrolled in a New York private school Fessenden but ate garbage in the streets or ran out of restaurants without paying the bill but those restaurants were now calling the police when seeing me on Fifth Avenue. I had to forget that the tall bald man with blonde hair accompanied my own father into my awful quarters with one lightbulb. I was hiding under the bathtub pretending I was dead. This awful man was no one I ever wished seeing again. I had been forced to play Russian roulette and seen two fellow American have their brains blown out.

I was well on my way to forget my awful experiences and ride high up the mountainside on the chairlift sometimes with Penny Hall, the daughter of the other owners of Tenney Mountain, Sam and Bernice Hall. I wanted to be a ski racer again, not a spy. I had never wanted to be a spy, it was not in my nature at all. My own father had instigated all this with that awful blond man. I wanted to forget them both and win the Junior National Ski Championships and be named to the U.S. Development Ski Team.

I did in Bend, Oregon in mid-March. After narrowly losing the downhill to Frederick Lounsberry of New York State, I won the giant slalom next day beating Ray Miller of Utah. I was a ski racer again. I was now on the long road home to being just me, myself and I

ST. FRIEND

(Have Confidence in God)

Trust that the God you pray to has ears

Have confidence in your God whose knowledge far surpasses your own

That He will deliver you from evil if you ask to be delivered

He will make you victorious in this your new day

For underfoot of the righteous is the Holy Land

Where you are now standing is where He has intended you to be

If there is danger He will instruct you to run away

It is not a safe place the earth and that is why you are given feet

That you might flee the tornado and outrun the flood

Your people are those who surround you daily, your friends

If they stand in the distance they have lost confidence in you

Why should they doubt that God protects us all?

His very angels are at work directing the daily traffic

To make you safe on your travels here in this dangerous world

He will not deliver you to the enemy while you still have a mission

To glorify His name among the people in many faraway places

The tree cannot flee from the lumberjack, take heed you are no tree

You have learned to read the newspaper, you see new clouds on the horizon

The wind is shifting so set your sails to accommodate our new tempest

Where you are standing you are meant to stand and where you travel

You are meant to travel to make new friends

Because perhaps your old friends are jealous of the success God has granted you some

You cannot bring them all with you, only those that love you

They hear God when you speak you mention God

You mention that God shall direct us to save ourselves because

Because God is with us now we are His people

Due to the remission of sin by the sacrifice of the Lamb who has died

For us in our place that we may feast and live at least until tomorrow

That is entirely a different day when we may be asked to sacrifice our own greed once again

In order to serve others, in order to follow like sheep or maybe to lead like the pastor

I am sorry and apologize to every friend I left behind, I did not serve you better

I was egocentric serving myself and perhaps not a good listener to your plea for help

So now we are each alone and no longer together as a team

Please come back to me if you hear my voice then be reassured

I have not forgotten you, I think of you and remember the good times

Our conversations to break the silence because God did not want us to be alone forever

He has gathered us here to be together in this His synogue His temple His chapel His cathedral

Or beneath this great pine tree to shade us or an oak

Here in the house of the Lord where you live, because if God cannot live here also in your home, neither shall you

Have confidence in God that He resides here with you if you obey His commandments

Worship no other God before Me says your God

You left your former friends because they heard a distant drummer somewhere

Not everyone can sing your song but keep singing anyway

Because God hears you and delights in your joy, your God reinforces you even if you are a hermit

Elijah fled the city and all the people to sit under a small shade tree in the desert

Where God spoke to him said,

"Get up and go, Elijah go prophesize the very good news that salvation is near for those who repent

Yes let us repent our wicked ways and come together as one people united not divided

Let us rejoin the circle of God's love given to us through us to rejoin hearts and hands

We can rebuild these lasting friendships to serve one another and the common good.

Not just our own selfish needs because you my friend are the best investment I ever made

God is my friend as well because He directed me in your direction

MY ST. FRIEND

(Have Confidence in God).

My friend who is more precious than wine, if I have lost you then let me drink wine and remember just how precious our time together

Trust that the God you pray to has ears

Have confidence in your God whose knowledge far surpasses your own

That He will deliver you from evil if you ask to be delivered

He will make you victorious in this your new day

For underfoot of the righteous is the Holy Land

Where you are now standing is where He has intended you to be

If there is danger He will instruct you to run away

It is not a safe place the earth and that is why you are given feet

That you might flee the tornado and outrun the flood

Your people are those who surround you daily, your friends

If they stand in the distance they have lost confidence in you

Why should they doubt that God protects us all?

His very angels are at work directing the daily traffic

To make you safe on your travels here in this dangerous world

He will not deliver you to the enemy while you still have a mission

To glorify His name among the people in many faraway places

The tree cannot flee from the lumberjack, take heed you are no tree

You have learned to read the newspaper, you see new clouds on the horizon

The wind is shifting so set your sails to accommodate our new tempest

Where you are standing you are meant to stand and where you travel

You are meant to travel to make new friends

Because perhaps your old friends are jealous of the success God has granted you some

You cannot bring them all with you, only those that love you

They hear God when you speak you mention God

You mention that God shall direct us to save ourselves because

Because God is with us now we are His people

Due to the remission of sin by the sacrifice of the Lamb who has died

For us in our place that we may feast and live at least until tomorrow

That is entirely a different day when we may be asked to sacrifice our own greed once again

In order to serve others, in order to follow like sheep or maybe to lead like the pastor

I am sorry and apologize to every friend I left behind, I did not serve you better

I was egocentric serving myself and perhaps not a good listener to your plea for help

So now we are each alone and no longer together as a team

Please come back to me if you hear my voice then be reassured

I have not forgotten you, I think of you and remember the good times

Our conversations to break the silence because God did not want us to be alone forever

He has gathered us here to be together in this His synogue His temple His chapel His cathedral or mosque (or should we invent our own religion?)

Or beneath this great pine tree to shade us or an oak

Here in the house of the Lord where you live, because if God cannot live here also in your home, neither shall you

Have confidence in God that He resides here with you if you obey His commandments

Worship no other God before Me says your God

You left your former friends because they heard a distant drummer somewhere

Not everyone can sing your song but keep singing anyway

Because God hears you and delights your joy, your God reinforces you even if you are a hermit

Elijah fled the city and all the people to sit under a small shade tree in the desert

Where God spoke to him said,

"Get up and go, Elijah go prophesize the very good news that salvation is near for those who repent

Yes let us repent our wicked ways and come together as one people united not divided

Let us rejoin the circle of God's love given to us through us to rejoin hearts and hands

We can rebuild these lasting friendships to serve one another and the common good

Not just our own selfish needs because you my friend are the best investment I ever made

God is my friend as well because He directed me in your direction

He has given me that I may lay down my own life for you

You are thankful and gracious to have a friend like me sent from God

I am thankful and gracious to be able to wash your feet lovingly

Thank you for being my friend, even though we barely met and talked but a few days

Our destinies on earth pulled us apart into different directions, even so

May God gladly reunite us one day, let us hope so

THE GREATEST BATTLE TO END GLOBAL WARMING

Please be on our team! Stand with us...

It is mankind's own greed to consume fossil fuel without limit that has gotten us into this mess. It will take a team effort by us all to contain our reckless endangerment of our planet.

At every toll booth on every highway in every western nation, one car with a single occupant driver should volunteer to pay one extra dollar above the standard toll fee or fill out a required form declaring why he or she does not wish to join our team effort to save (White Christmas) our white winters.

This is not about I or me: this is about us and future generations, whether or not there will be any. Existential man's greed may cause the extinction of his species.

So I am asking you to please join our ski and skate team at least in spirit and consider carpooling and sharing your ride with another team member. We will be able to do this all together, united in spirit, on the same page on this winning team together.

It was not God's intention that we live alone. Man should not be alone and lonely so God created Eve etcetera. Selfishness is destroying us.

(Written driving from Rhode Island homeward through Franconia Notch watching skiers on Cannon Mountain, an endangered species in an endangered business, winter tourism)

Printed in the United States
By Bookmasters